WAR CHILD

C. P. CLARKE

War Child - Attack On The Village

War Child, Volume 1

C. P. Clarke

Published by C. P. Clarke, 2023.

For details of other books in the series and for how you can read
material by C. P. Clarke for free see details at the end of the book.
If you enjoy reading this story, then please leave a review:
amazon.com/author/c.p.clarke
If you would like to be on my mailing list for updates on new material
and offers or you'd like to contact me directly then email:
info@cpclarke-author.com

Author's note:

This book is far removed from my previous works. When I started writing it I didn't think it would weave into the wider story of alternate realities that cross over into my other novels, however as I drew toward the end of writing this story there seemed to be a natural way of bringing in an old character and the influence of the mysterious conglomerate controlling the events on the world stage. You'll have to read to the end of part three to see the links in my thinking, but for those who have read my other books, you won't be disappointed.

As for War Child, the concept of this came about as I sat talking to a game designer friend of mine who was looking for an idea for a game based off a novel. As we batted ideas around the table I proposed the idea which led to this book.

Writing the storyline in conjunction with a game designer has been a challenge as the pace of the story has had to keep up with the expectation of playable scenes within a computer game. This has meant that the perspectives of characters has been limited and the action plentiful, all the while trying to maintain a believable storyline.

Fortunately for the storyline, and indeed the original concept, I was able to draw on personal knowledge and experience of the region in which it is set. The whole story is set in Africa, in a non-descript country torn apart by civil war. Into this world of pain is born a boy who must battle his way through the hardships of war and death, the suffering of abduction and the torment of soldiers who wish to use him as a pawn in their own malicious feud.

Very sadly much of what I draw on for this story is all too real in many parts of Africa. Yes, there are elements of the book which are pure fantasy, crossing genres to add elements of battle play for the game with creatures that can't be killed, but on the whole the desperate plight of child soldiers and the brutality they face is very real.

I named this book War Child as it seemed appropriate at the very early stages. It was only once I'd written about a third of the first section that I remembered reading a book of a similar title many years ago before departing for a mission trip to Africa. The book was written by a rapper from Sudan who had found acclaim as an artiste having finally been set free to begin a new life having lived for years as a child soldier. The book is called War Child – A boy soldier's story, by Emmanuel Jal. If you have to decide between reading my book or reading his, then read his! It is an amazing true story that will open up your eyes to the horrors facing some children in Africa today.

I hope you enjoy this story, which for the purposes of the game is set as a trilogy. Hopefully the game itself will follow on day.

C. P. Clarke February 2018

Game storyline based on an original idea by C. P. Clarke and Robert Miller

Part One
Attack on the Village

1

The heartlands of Africa have been my home for so long now that I have grown comfortable with their surroundings, and with the people. I have let my guard down at long last. I am settled. I am making a difference and doing good work here. I am happy, and for the first time in my life content. But I should have known better than to give in to this false sense of security. How could I ever think I could be safe here?

As far as medical facilities go ours is pretty basic. Four walls and a roof, two beds, a handful of wooden chairs bought from a nearby village, two long tables to work from and one lockable cabinet for supplies. It isn't much, but compared to the rest of our small village it is all a luxury.

Small round mud huts arranged in concentric circles in family units spread across the flat land bordered by the rising forest on all sides. A few trees sprout out within the village camp are used for shelter from the equatorial heat that scorch this mid-African terrain when the heavy rains aren't falling.

These humble and peaceful people share everything. Not just possessions: children, parental responsibility, grandparents, food, clothes, and yes the communal toilet huts that serve them all; it is one of the few structures (including the medical centre) that has a door, only ours is the only one with a secure and properly hung frame.

As well as providing medical care we also act as the drop off and distribution centre for any food aid that comes in from the city or aid agencies. So remote are we from the main towns that few can locate us by the dirt track that weaves through the dense woodland. Being so shut off I often make regular supply runs in the truck (one of only two working vehicles that service the village), leaving Jenny and Benjamin in the hands of the tribe we have come to love so much.

We had been coming back and forth to the region for almost eight years before setting up the clinic as a permanent feature in the village and moving here as a long term project to help these people and those in the surrounding area. We have earned their trust, and those of other towns and villages flock to us, often making the long journey on foot through troubled and dangerous countryside to seek the basic aid we offer. We are funded by well-meaning sponsors in more favourable corners of the world, and the medical supplies are donated by big pharmaceutical corporations who do it out of an obligation to ease their guilty consciences over the extortionate fees they charge the African governments for the same medical essentials.

Benjamin was only four when Jenny first met him here in the village, and she had agreed almost immediately that he was special. I'd been telling her so for years, ever since I'd started sponsoring him soon after his birth through a charity that sought to help young orphaned children in the area. The charity had long gone bust but that hadn't stopped me from supporting the boy I'd come to love as my own son.

Many kids in the village have English sounding names, whether a throwback to colonialism or an attempt to fit in with Western culture I couldn't say. What I do know is that they are very proud of their God given names and pronounce every syllable with a smile.

Benjamin isn't ours by blood, but he is the closest to a son we are ever likely to get. There are many orphans in the village, cast offs from a civil war that has left a generation roaming the wilds fending for themselves; children of rape and desolated communities. The war is over, but the terror still reigns with rebel groups randomly attacking peaceful settlements for no other apparent reason other than that they can.

Benjamin, like the other kids in his position, has found a home with the help of Westerners like us, only he was fortunate enough to have us keep returning year after year, investing in his life and that of the community.

It had been Jenny's idea for us to move out here long term. She had the medical expertise and I the local knowledge and community and government contacts to make it work. I knew the trade routes. I knew the warring factions. I knew the ecology and the wildlife. In essence I knew how to survive here, and she trusted me to know how to keep her safe.

"Father," says the boy, growing strong and handsome as he breaks his teenage year and soon to be recognised among his peers as a man and no longer the helpless little orphan, "do we have time for football?"

As polite as ever Benjamin seeks permission from me to play with the other children. He knows the answer. There is never really an objection. What he is really asking without making it obvious is, when will lunch be ready?

"You have time, go play!"

"Thank you, Father." And off he runs to the far side of the village to the open ground on the edge of the huts where one or two trees are the only obstacles to skirt around as he and his friends, in their short sleeves and short pants, chase their ball of wrapped twine filled with discarded plastics, kicking with toughened bare feet.

He is gone no more than five minutes when the first unmistakable shots ring out, breaking the peace of the village so that all falls still in alarm, save for the birds that fly in a wild panic from the treetops.

"Stay here," I command Jenny on instinct. She heads to the cabinet and unlocks it and retrieves the shotgun we keep there. She knows the drill. Victoria, a woman from the village who helps out and is learning the ropes from Jenny, cowers behind her as she shuts the door behind me.

I draw my pistol and wait for the next shot to ring out and echo across the woodland so I can identify where it is coming from. It is off on the far side of the village, not where the boys are playing football but farther into the tree line where the well is and the water pump from which we all fill our yellow canisters.

I head off in that direction as panicked shouts rise in response of more gunfire.

Angry shouts of unrecognisable male voices cut in as I work my way through the circles of huts, going against the grain of fleeing peasants, confused and fearful. Then I smell it - the burning.

Suddenly my worst fears are awakened. The homes, the simple round mud huts that contain the entire wealth and possessions of these people are being set alight. I can smell the smoke rising. I can hear some of the men and women of the village trying to stand their ground and protect their own. I can hear the screams and wails as the odd shot sings through the air.

There isn't as much shooting as you might expect - there never is. Many would have still been in their huts, caught unawares, the dried reed roofing catching quickly. Those that made it out were probably hacked down by an unknown number of machete wielding troops marching out of the forest.

I glimpse one or two green guerilla uniforms stepping out of their camouflaged backdrop, silently slaying the innocents. One woman I see is being dragged into an unlit hut after being punched unconscious. The soldier undoing the belt of his trousers as he takes her in.

Suddenly I am aware of the shouts, and the screams; from the villagers it is fear, and terror, and pain; from the soldiers it is bold and callous bellows of rage and the laughter of the insane.

I take aim to shoot but then hear the scream from the medical hut and the unmistakable sound of the shotgun blasting, once, twice, but no more.

I'd been lured away and now Jenny was in trouble and the village was burning around me. I just hoped Benjamin and the other children had sense enough to run for the woods in time.

I turn to the trees, prepared to run for cover as my father had taught me, but others aren't so sure. As our ball rolled out of play and we all stopped our jostling for position on the makeshift football pitch the first shots sounded, some of my playmates turned back to their homes.

I couldn't blame most of them, they were young; one was barely six, most were aged around ten or eleven, and a few were a couple of years older than me. The younger ones wanted the comfort and security of the community. The older ones thought they were old enough and big enough to fight to protect it.

I ran for cover. Not out of cowardice you understand, it's just that my father had given me specific instructions should the village ever get attacked.

I hit the trees running, a couple of others close on my heels. When I think we're far enough I stop and hunker down in the bushes and look for a place to peer back through the trees at the activity by the huts closest to where we had been playing.

The older boys had been captured quickly as they tried to skirt around the outside of the huts to reach the far side of the village quicker. A band of militia in khaki uniforms broke from the trees and pistol whipped them as they ran.

The younger boys froze in fright as they trailed behind and then on command lay down on the ground with their hands behind their heads. I thought they were going to be shot, but what happened next was much worse.

Two of the older boys are dragged to a tree and tied to it, one on either side. A third is stripped naked along with his sister who had been playing with us. The soldiers force him to abuse her. He begs not to. They beat him. Then they, the soldiers, four of them, rape them both in turn before shooting the boy and knocking the girl unconscious, which is unnecessary as she is clearly already numb and distant enough by this point.

A forth older boy is being held at gun point, he's been commanded not to react to anything he sees: not to the gunfire, not to the screams and shouts of the villagers they are blind to, not to the smoke rising and the crackle of flames as our homes burn, not to the brutalisation of his friends stood around him. He does as commanded - he just stands there, having unashamedly peed his pants.

I can see small fights breaking out within the village as the adults fight the soldiers. Some parents are screaming, desperate to reach the field where their children are being gathered together. The battles are short lived. The cries and shouts quickly silenced, and the resistance quashed with an unsympathetic and emotionless response of finality.

A couple of the ten year olds are instructed to stand up. The others told to sit and watch. The two standing are handed club-like sticks. I can't hear what is being said, but I can guess. The boys shake their heads. The two tied to the tree began to come around and then start screaming, but no one is coming to their aid; everyone has their own battles to fight.

The two younger boys continue to shake their heads. Aiming his pistol at the boy who has been commanded to just stand still the soldier speaks to the younger boys again. Hesitantly they move towards the tree and raise their clubs but refuse to swing them. The single shot burrows deep and flies out of the face of the boy standing still. He falls to the ground.

The soldier issues his instruction again. With tears streaming down their faces the boys began to strike the tree and the faces and bodies of those tied to it.

I look away appalled. That could have been me. I can feel the urine warming my crotch. I would have been surprised if those crouched with me had dry pants too.

I begin to back away, remembering my father's instructions to get as far away as possible, but as I turn three soldiers stand over us with their weapons raised at our heads, having crept up stealthily behind us.

The whites of the eyes are what stuns me into hesitation as the rebel soldier steps out from the side of the medical block appearing to be caught in some sort of trance as I race towards it. My mind can't quite comprehend what I am seeing in him, and I have no time to react to it as I am clumped from behind.

I awake inside where I had started. I have no idea how much time has elapsed, it could have been minutes since this ordeal began or it could have been hours. I am tied and gagged to a chair. Jenny isn't tied up but I can see from the red marks on her wrists that she had been, the coarse rope having torn into her skin where she had tried to loosen the bonds. Smeared dried blood edges the corner of her mouth, but that isn't the worst of it.

Her dress is torn and gaping to show her underwear has been removed, forcibly ripped off. I close my eyes and grit my teeth, a sickening bile rising in my throat as I vow there and then that if I survive this then I will make them pay.

I look across the room. In the background, behind the two armed soldiers who care little for hiding their faces and the crimes they've committed, most likely pleased with having spilt themselves on white flesh, grinning with pride at the atrocities they have brought upon this otherwise peaceful part of the world, lays Victoria. On one of the two hospital beds we'd been donated, and where she had worked tirelessly to help her people, she lay, her legs sprawled indecently, her eyes fixed and her face trapped in a painful spasm, her last breath having long expired. How she had died I can only guess, probably she resisted too hard, maybe her desire to preserve her dignity winning over that of self-preservation.

A third guard walks into the room, or maybe he had been there all along, I can't be sure. He steps out from behind me. He is tall and broad and carries the scars of scores of battles, one of which slices from his left eye across his nose to the right cheek. Flashes of this man riding above my wife, gyrating as he grins back at me, sweep back over my vision as

I realise this isn't the first time I've awoken in this room. They have me drugged and have been waking me periodically to torture me with the horrors of what they are doing to Jenny while I watch helpless to alter the outcome. I try to block out the mental image.

This man is a monster. A giant in size but also in demeanor. He is intelligent and experienced. This is no foot soldier, this is the leader, and what's more - I know his name.

He grabs Jenny by the hair and drags her forward so that she kneels in front of me. Then he raises his pistol to Jenny's head. There is pleading in her eyes as tearily she begs me to help. I say nothing, not that I am able to with the gag in my mouth, but I try to comfort her with a final look of peace to send her where she needs to go.

He is looking at me as he pulls the trigger, but I won't satisfy him with the return stare of hatred that he desires. Instead I close my eyes as my wife's blood and brains splatters across my face, and I keep them closed.

The room is still and silent. I wait. Eventually I open my eyes to see him still standing there holding her by her hair. Only now he is waiting for me to watch as he swings at her neck with a machete, letting her body topple forward, her blood spurting out at me. He then tosses her head into my blood-soaked lap, his laugh echoing in my head as I fight the urge to vomit as my senses dissolve into a dizzying spin around me.

I am numb for what follows. I have a sense of what is happening but am too distant from it, as though I am floating out of my body looking down upon proceedings.

We, the survivors (if that's what you could term us as) are rounded up and placed in restraints. The men placed in one truck, the women in another, and the children in yet another. I know the routine, it is an old guerilla tactic: send the men to work hacking down pathways or building temporary camps and then kill them when they are no longer required or became too much of a liability to keep guard over; the women would be taken as brides, some would be mutilated, their noses and lips cut off to prevent them wanting to return to their people, some would fall pregnant, and nearly all would contract HIV Aids from the repeated abuse; the children would be conditioned, tortured and forced to commit atrocious acts upon each other to dehumanise them in order to create the next wave of soldiers loyal to their cause.

At least Benjamin would have escaped. He would have run, or so I hope. But then none of my plans to keep us safe have worked out so far.

As the trucks they had brought with them pull out of the charred remains of the village I try to study the faces onboard. I can't see for most of the rugged journey up into the hills away from the nearest big town, but where the road forks the trucks stop. The women and children are being taken one way and the men, me included, another. My truck draws alongside the children, and there pushed up against the side as a final taunt, is Benjamin.

He looks at me, my face covered in the dried and crusted blood of his mother. I call out his name as the truck begins to move off. I hear him call for me, hear him beg for my help. I wrestle with my restraints and jostle for fighting space, but once again I am knocked unconscious, left with the dreams of my screaming family whom I would never see again.

2

I don't know how long I'd been out for. Joshua had tried to bring me round by tapping my foot occasionally. I noticed it as I eventually drew myself away from Jenny's warm embrace as we slow danced on our wedding day; she was beautiful, staring at me with such innocence and trust that I would keep her safe.

Joshua tilts his head to the armed guard sat on the end of the bench leaning against the wooden slats of the truck. He hangs one finger from his closed fist between his legs and then looks the other way to the driver's cab and drops two more fingers. I nod my understanding and stay silent as I look to who else is with us.

There are no young men amongst us, no elderly either. The young hotheads would have been too much of an unpredictable threat and would have been massacred in the attack. The old, too infirm to be of any use, most likely left alone to salvage what they could from the village. It isn't in the rebel group's interest to wipe the people out completely, they need survivors to spread the fear that upholds their reputation.

Moses and John sit uncomfortably at the end closest to the rear of the driver's cab. Moses has a machete wound to his leg which is tied badly in a poor attempt to stop the bleeding. Unless he gets urgent medical attention it will get infected quickly. I've seen wounds like his before, if he doesn't bleed out he will die a slow painful death as the poisoned wound overtakes his body; he will last maybe two weeks at most, probably less with forced labour. He will need his brother John sat next to him to carry his burden. Neither will be in a position to make a break for it.

Another Moses sits next to me. It is a popular name; many names being chosen to reflect the religious background of one of the main two religions that have caused conflict in the surrounding nations over the years. His parents had been Christian, but Abdul's, who is squeezed between him and the guard sat against the rear flap of the truck, were Muslim. Neither men were in conflict with each other and lived happily alongside each other in the village where no religious animosity intruded or interfered in village life. Abdul is strong and tenacious, but Moses I know to be in character weak and cowardly. If we made a break for it, Abdul would most likely get Moses killed.

A seventh man sits with us, like the others he is aged in his late 30's or early 40's (it is always difficult to judge their exact ages, and most keep no record of the actual date they were born) but he too is of no use. George is a simpleton, not so much the village idiot, but having had a difficult birth he had beaten the odds to survive to adulthood in a harsh environment with mental restrictions. In the Western world he would have received the medical care he needed but most likely would have been ostracised by society, but here in the heart of Africa it was the opposite: he was loved and accepted by the community. Physically able, and easily pliable, he would be an easy tool for a manual labour workforce but a liability in an attempted escape plan.

I look up at the world through the open roof of the truck and at the darkening sky above where the clouds are beginning to cover the dwindling sun falling to the horizon. The day is too short, the weather unsteady. We are moving east and descending, trees climbing to overhang the truck in a tunnel of shade. I look back down to see marks in the dust by Joshua's feet, scratch marks he has made with his toes indicating the turns of a map. He has been charting our course. We may have been driving for a while, but we were going in circles. He spins his finger to confirm my thoughts.

They don't want us knowing where they were taking us, but I have a fair idea.

Joshua joins his fingers together in a peak. I nod. We had circled around the forest to come around to the almost inaccessible base of the mountain that rises out of the forest into the protected national park. I had often thought that the guerillas had a base there, now I knew.

If we were heading there, then where were they taking the children? A training camp most likely. There were plenty of them, adapted from already raided villages. I try to picture the road they had taken. I try to picture the camps and villages along the route. I try to picture where they could have taken Benjamin. I have to get back to him. I have to rescue him. But first I have to get us away from the guards and get the villagers to safety.

3

I know the drill, yelling and shouting and riling the dogs all night to ensure we can't sleep. They put us all in one small tent, closed so that we can't see what they are doing. No mats. No blankets. The occasional kick of the canvas if they see a body bulging enough to target. If we need to relieve ourselves we are allowed out, chained to a tree in front of the tent opening which is held agape to ensure an audience.

I have a weak bladder. I care little for the spectators staring, they aren't my concern.

Eight men guard the camp at any one time during the night, which means there would be at least another four during the day. Ours isn't the only tent. There are three, with up to eight men in each, with four of the guards sat around a fire in the middle and dogs tied to trees at the rear of each. That gives a maximum of 23 captives to 12 militia. The odds are getting better, depending upon the condition of the prisoners I have yet to lay eyes on.

Two guards hunker down by a tree on a two hour rotation whilst the remaining two guard the road. There is one vehicle that enters the camp during the night, a returning scout I think at first, but then I hear the clatter of riffles being unloaded into one of the two wooden shacks that has been constructed. My guess is these had been built by the other teams that lay sleeping in the other tents.

Two foundations have been dug for brick structures but haven't progressed any further, telling me this is a new camp and is intended as being a long-term base. They are getting bold enough to make permanent footholds in this part of the forest, which means their numbers are growing along with their confidence. There is a brick compactor I can just make out glinting yellowy orange firelight off its rusted frame. They will set us to work making bricks and then hauling them to the foundations, and then will come the mixing of the cement, the *thabiti*. It will be back braking work, work some in my group wouldn't survive.

The delivery driver doesn't stay. He probably has a whole shipment he is dropping off at the various camps. Once again my mind drifts as to where those camps are - where Benjamin has been taken.

In the cramped conditions of our tent in the darkness of night as we huddle together, I map out the vehicles, the huts, the guards, the dogs, the likely new arrivals at dawn. I ponder what the huts contain: guns, radios, rations, maps? I need access to what is inside, but first I need to get the prisoners free.

Morning comes. As expected a small 4x4 jeep arrives with fresh blood. Only then are we were hauled out at gun point. A chunk of bread and a bottle of dirty water to pass around between us is all the generosity we are granted. This is a good sign; you don't waste food and water on those you intend to kill.

Moses looks worse in the daylight than I had expected him to be. I'd heard his groans and grunting during the night but now I can see him I can tell by the pallor of his skin that his wound is worse than I had initially thought and is most likely already infected. If we are to flee it will have to be soon.

The night guards will be weary and eager for rest. The replacements still dopey from a good night's sleep. I will have to make my move early. Once committed there will be no turning back. The alarm will be raised quickly and reinforcements will pile in.

I get my first good look at the other prisoners over breakfast before we are all marched over to a heap of sand and mud mix next to the brick compactor. There are only five in each tent. That means there are only seventeen of us. Including Moses, three look to have injuries.

We can all fit in one truck, but I will need to disable a minimum of three guards before I can get to the shack to get what I need. I can count on Joshua to follow my lead, maybe even Abdul, but I have my doubts about the others.

I have to make a decision: go for what I want in the shack, or settle for getting the villagers clear of the danger zone. In the end I know what is the right thing to do, I just hope I can get them all out alive.

"Mzungu!" There is only one person in the camp that can answer that call. I turn to have a shovel thrown at me by a guard. They have chosen me for the first stint of back braking mixing of materials. Others will be sent to fetch water from the drums that I hadn't been able to see in the dark during the night. It makes sense: tire out the strongest in the group early. But they don't know what I know, what I can see, and they have just handed me the weapon I needed.

"Mzungu!" another shouts pointing to the dirt pile, showing his ignorance of the English language but knowing that all white men that live here answer to the label of their skin colour.

I can see the slight slither of brown through the grass towards the path, the dart of black tongue as it searches out a place to curl up in the rising light of day, and can I tell the guard has failed to see it. It is unlikely I will get another opportunity as fortuitous as this. I catch Joshua's eye, give a slight nod of my head. He reads me well and I see him look to Abdul and give the same nod.

Stepping forward it all happens quickly. Scooping the mamba up in the shovel I fling it at the guard by the dirt pile and swing back round with the back end of the spade smashing the guard behind me in the face and then using the edge of it to cut down into his neck. There is no chance for mercy, there is no time.

Snatching his rifle, I turn on those closest to the villagers and fire three quick and direct shots. Joshua and Abdul and one of the men from the other group reach for their weapons, leaving me to take aim on the two guards in the distance by the trucks.

Snake-man is convulsing, wriggling about on the ground, fighting a losing battle with the venomous black mamba that sees him as the aggressor. Unsurprisingly no one goes for his gun.

Five down, seven left, all in a matter of seconds. I take out the two by the trucks. Five left. I have to keep them away from the radio and the hut.

The shots will bring soldiers from near and far and we need to hit the road quickly; we won't get far unless I can seal off the road behind us.

We get lucky. Someone is looking down on us it would seem. One of the guards was relieving himself, having parked his rifle out of reach. Joshua catches him with a succession of bullets as he stumbles with his pants down.

Four.

Half of the villagers had ducked to the ground when the shooting started. Those able and alert enough to read the signs crouched low and then scuttled like rats over toward the trucks, using the water drums and trees as cover. Reaching the edge of a truck they turned back wanting to know the next move. Half the group hadn't joined them and the likelihood was that none of them have driven a truck before.

Joshua and Abdul laid down fire as they tried to cover those hunkered down on the ground.

I run, slamming my back into the side of one of the wooden shacks. Shots blast out from inside, splintering the slats and narrowly missing me as they paint a new pattern of permanent decor. The holes created are big enough for me to see in but I can only glimpse as I crouch low knowing I can't stay there to be a target. I fire back into the wall as I run, hoping that my blind shooting will hit one of the two men I guess to be inside.

Beneath the crackle of gunfire I can hear the hiss and static of a radio and an excitable voice demanding assistance in Swahili.

Our time is up. I wave over to Joshua to get the others to the trucks. We need to go now before the road gets cut off ahead of us.

Joshua encourages them to run for the trucks as Abdul keeps firing. Those at the vehicles are already climbing in the back of one.

The camp falls eerily silent. Abdul is out of bullets, so are the two guards he was shooting at. I edge around the corner of the huts and take them out.

Two left, and they are in the hut with all the riffles and ammo.

I sprint for the truck and jump in the driver's seat - the key is in the ignition. I start the engine and check the side mirror to check the progress of the others. Most are in but a few stragglers are trailing behind. Abdul rushes back to help them.

The door of the hut bursts open. I'd missed both of them as I'd fired into the shack. Now they both run out and kneel, taking aim on the stragglers.

Before I can open the door to fire back at them Moses with the wounded leg catches a bullet clean in the chest and falls flat to the ground. Abdul pushes the others forward to the truck but takes one to the head for his trouble.

Joshua draws their fire with his last two shots, buying me enough time to exit the vehicle and take a measured moment. I fire twice. Both hit their target. Both are fatal.

We are clear of the village, but not out of danger. I consider making a run for the shack and grabbing what I need, but I know every second will count if we are to escape to a main road or village. The truck will be a big target on a small road.

Scrambling into the back Joshua is yelling at my hesitance as I take a couple of steps away from the truck. We could use the weapons, the maps.

Joshua yells again, jumps out and grabs my arm and pushes me back towards the cab and climbs in with me. He has served in the regular army as a young man fighting guerillas such as these. He knows their tactics just as well as I do.

I jump back in the cab, release the handbrake and power the truck onto the dirt track, carving a hidden path through the trees.

We drive for twenty minutes without incident before Joshua states that he thinks he recognises where we are. He knows the region better than I. There is a town nearby on the crest of a valley, surrounded by suburbs of communities. It is likely it is this town that attracted the rebel group to the area in the first place. It was likely they would be looking long term to use it as a stronghold to control access to the base of the mountain range and the transport routes across it.

The lack of soldiers in our path is a good sign. It means their camps are more spread out. They will catch up with us eventually so long as we stayed on the road.

John, sitting next to Joshua on one of the two passenger seats in the front cab, wanting the distraction from the loss of Moses and all else that has transpired over the last day, reaches over and turns on the radio. A political businessman, Gerard Rubekki, is protesting against the rebel skirmishes into mountains from across the border. The state owned station presenter starts questioning him about the dangers of Western oil companies drilling in the national parks. I turn it off. We've all heard it before, and I don't want the distraction of extra noise that could block out an approaching vehicle.

I ask Joshua if he can find the town on foot. If anyone is to lead these people to safety it would be him. I have other priorities.

Accepting the charge, I stop the truck and Joshua unloads the villagers, huddling them together off the road. We part ways here with a promise that I will come back to find them if I can. They will be safe if they can reach the town. I promise them I will return their families if I can find them. Joshua, and those from our village know me, Joshua the best. They know I am a man of my word. They know my attachment to Benjamin. They also know they have no other choice.

We say our goodbyes. I wait until they disappear into the forest and then I drive the truck on for another mile or so before ditching it into the first gap in the trees I think it will fit into. I slam it into the biggest tree head first, bracing myself for the impact as the radiator bursts open with the crumpling of the bonnet. A thin line of steam rises and fizzles out. I stop to listen for any reaction to the crash. The birds that had flown up in panic settle back down. All else is calm. I step away, abandoning the vehicle. My hope is that the patrols I know are coming will find it, think we had crashed and then walked off into the trees or along the path, aimlessly searching safety, walking away from the danger zone we had left and in the opposite direction of the town they didn't know we knew existed.

Shadowing the path I keep to the tree line, back-tracking to the camp we had just left.

4

The sounds of cicadas, birds, and even the odd monkey high up in the trees are enough to keep me on edge. I shy away from the roadside where I suspect heavy vehicles will come rumbling along at any moment, but treading this thin narrow trail of natural cover created by the wildlife, which hides the potential hidden enemy beyond in the trees, jitters my nerves more than facing a full on assault of soldiers out in the open.

I know the guerillas are all well adept at hiding deep in the forest and have perfected the mimicking calls of nature. For this reason the long walk back in silence, unarmed, listening to the tread of my own feet as the humidity rises with the sun, haunts me. I crave an open warrior to challenge me and channel the adrenalin racing through my veins pounding from my over excited and fearful heart. Fear is a great energiser. Fear is a keen observer. Fear keeps me focused.

I carry the AK47 I had requisitioned at the camp; it is the common weapon of both the regular army and just about every other rebel group to rise up in the African nations. The Russian rifle is cheap and easy to acquire, and the ammunition is plentiful, and few military arms have the resources to afford anything else. Unfortunately, like the weapon Joshua had wielded, I too am out of bullets. I carry it for show. If I am lucky I can use it to bluff for a greater position, or at the very least have a momentary standoff.

I'm a pretty good judge of distances so I know I am fairly close to the camp when I hear the truck rumbling down the track behind me. I conceal myself behind a bush that allows me a safe view of the dusty road yet provides the secure trunk of a tree to my back.

I have been crouched low for less than a minute when the growing thunder of the engine, a cattle hauler similar to the one I'd driven earlier from the sound of it, becomes the least curious noise around me. Behind me I can hear a rustling, a slow stamping of footfall squelching the mud and crunching the downed twigs in a meandering path around the trees towards the road. Within moments a villager comes into view.

I assume he is from a nearby settlement, his clothes ragged, his feet donned in poorly fitting but well-worn leather slip-ons. Two things give him away as being aligned with the rebels: the low hanging AK47 with its brown butt reaching up into his armpit as he walks, and the curious egg whites of his eyes that glaze over his vision.

I've seen eyes like that only once before, back in our village before I'd been clobbered and knocked unconscious. I didn't understand it then, and still don't even now. But at least this time I can observe it a bit closer without the fear of being struck.

He has no idea I am here. He can't see me. In fact, I am surprised he can see anything at all as the milky white glaze covers his pupils.

He reaches the verge just before the truck comes into view and stands waiting. The driver slows on his approach just enough for the villager, for he isn't a trained soldier nor part of the regular rebel group, to latch onto the outside wooden slats, get a foot up and hold on. He isn't the only one, four others are clinging to the outside of the truck, and there are at least another ten sat uncomfortably inside. Of those I can see clearly, at least three have eyes similar to the one that has blindly walked past me.

I don't concern myself too much with the apparent deformity in the eyes. There are many strange diseases and unclassified genetic markers that breed within the local inhabitants, many caused by malnutrition, although none like this have ever drawn our attention at the medical centre we'd set up. Jenny had dealt with plenty of cataracts in some of the older folk, assessing them, advising on them, but unfortunately unable to cure them - they needed surgical intervention and a simple procedure we simply weren't set up to perform. But this isn't cataracts - I know the difference.

My mind is focused more on trying to calculate what I am walking into. One truck with up to twenty armed men. It would possibly pick up one or two more en route. There were maybe a dozen or more that could have already made their way into the camp on foot from nearby settlements or outposts. How many of them were trained rebels and how many were coerced villagers remains to be seen. I don't want to take on the locals unless I have to; they too are victims in all this.

I figure I am less than ten minutes out. I don't want to approach the camp from the roadside. I need to drift east, swing in from the rear of the camp, the ground rises steadily there giving me a slightly elevated view from which to assess the challenge. I want to drop in, raid the huts for anything useful and slip out unnoticed if possible. I know it is a big ask and the odds of it going down that way are slim, which is why I also have Plan B mapped out in the back of my mind.

Circling the camp takes me an extra half hour, which is risking more men in the fight if it comes to it, but approaching from the road would be too risky. I doubt they will be expecting any of us to double back, we were making a break for freedom after all, but the road would be watched nonetheless. I couldn't risk taking on an armed platoon at the camp entrance with possible re-enforcements driving in at my six.

Looking down now at the camp from my viewpoint I know immediately Plan A is a no go and Plan B would be in full effect. I will have to prioritise my actions:

Objective 1: acquire either ammunition for the weapon I carried or someone else's firearm; whichever is easier.

Objective 2: take out the four guards outside the first hut that contains the radio and disable transmissions and gather intel.

Objective 3: take out the two guards outside hut number two and retrieve as much intel and weapons from within as possible.

Objective 4: acquire transport (there are two trucks: the one I'd seen bringing in troops and the one we'd left behind) and get the hell out of there in one piece.

Of course, by the time I've achieved Objective 1 I am certain to be in a rush to reach Objective 4 as the whole camp will have been alerted to my presence, which leaves me with the unstated objective of taking out as many rebels as possible.

It is while I am mulling this over that the cold barrel of a rifle is pushed against the back of my neck.

I freeze. Whoever it is behind me is stealthier than I'd have given any of the soldier's credit for. Clearly I've been underestimating their skills.

Holding my hands wide, slowly I rise to my feet, aware that I am still hidden from view of the camp by dense foliage. I turn cautiously hoping there is only one of them. There is. A lone soldier wearing half fatigues, a loose fitting camouflaged waistcoat that isn't done up and khaki combat trousers with a gun belt and dagger hanging from his waist. His eyes are clear, normal, but glazed with the sickness I've seen in many a rebel soldier in the past. With some it is alcohol or drugs, many chew khatt which renders them 90% zombie dead weight when posted remotely away from their commanders. Either this one is recovering from a bender or he has a disease I don't want to catch.

He gestures for me to drop my rifle, something I am happy to do. I want both hands free. I am counting on him being slow to react. His finger isn't on the trigger but both hands are on the trunk of his weapon. Gracefully I sidestep him, grab his left hand on top of the rifle and pull him forward off balance, reaching in with my other hand and tugging his blade free of his belt. His rifle is attached via a strap which is hung over his head and arm. Before he has a chance to react I pulled on his rifle so hard that the strap pulls him low so that anything he attempts to yell is swallowed by his inability to suck in a breath. Taking advantage of his low posture I thrust down with his own knife into the back of his neck.

The whole motion takes less than a couple of seconds. The soldier falls, slowly eased down by my hand. He is dead and I am now in possession of his rifle, his knife, and his sidearm. Objective 1 achieved.

There are fresh drum barrels stacked by the tree line. All are empty bar one containing dirty drinking water which one of the four guarding the radio hut saunters over to, cups his hand in and splashes his face. He gives his face an extra rub as if to wake himself up. I wait until he turns back around before making a break from my vantage point, sliding down to the tree line, crouching low in a diagonal from the hut to the drums knowing that most of my route will be covered. So long as they all hold their positions for the next couple of minutes I will stay out of direct line of sight and approach the central hut from the rear by the drums.

I scurry like a fast moving jungle tarantula, feeling the footfall of prey and seeking shelter behind the nearest object that provides shadow. I linger behind the metal drum, catching my breath and listening for any change in pattern of the soldiers. There is none. So far so good.

I dare to raise my head above the rim of the barrels. The four men on guard duty are chatting over a smoke. They don't appear to be highly trained or disciplined but do appear to be part of the regular militia and not local villagers coerced into the fight.

I figure I need a distraction and am wondering how I can divert their attention to the woods on the left when just at that moment a heavy crunch of leaves and snapping branches trails a path from that very direction.

I tip my head briefly to see four men, three with glazed over moonbeam eyes, and one without bringing up the rear as if having railroaded the others.

The four at the hut look across also, two breaking away to welcome the new arrivals. I take my chance.

I leave the rifle on the ground, I won't need it, I am still aiming for a stealthy approach.

I gorilla stomp towards the hut, my knuckles scraping the dirt floor, the odd bunches of grass tickling the back of my hand holding the hunting knife poised to strike. I leap up like a small child reaching for a piggyback from his father, only as my hand wraps around the neck of the tall dark-skinned parental figure does it slice at the throat of the wannabe baby-father. I spin quickly with the same blade, using the first man as cover as I hide my movement between him and the hut wall, and drive the blade up into the chin of the second man.

I now have six men approaching me in single file, none of whom have yet spotted what I've just done. I grab the rifle of the second man as I prop him up in a standing position with my knife, my left hand taking his weight as blood drips down my arm. Relieving him of his weapon I let him fall. I fall with him onto one knee and then line up my shots.

Six shots ring out in succession. Six men fall in a line. By the time anyone can react to the gunfire I am already inside the hut hoping all outside are looking out to the trees in confusion of the direction of the assailant they can't see. I doubt any of them are bright enough to do the math on the number of shots and the number of bodies.

Inside I am relieved to hear the gunfire ripping apart the trees to the left. If I am lucky they will take some of their own out in the crossfire. I guess I have about 90 seconds before they realise the radio shack is compromised.

Unfortunately, I am not alone inside. Two men sit at a desk. The one with his hand on the radio transmitter I disposed of quickly with a couple of shots disguised from outside. But the other one is on me too quickly and I have no room to close the distance with the rifle. He kicks out with a front snap kick which sends me flying against the far wall. This one has hand to hand combat training, a common asset in the jungle squads, but few have actual martial arts skills as this one appears to have; a lame kick is easy to tell apart from someone who knows what he is doing. I don't have time to tussle with this guy.

I push off from the wall and thrust forward with my elbow. I miss. He sidesteps and counters to my chin. He catches me, not full on but a clip enough to cause me to wobble. I go down, but only halfway. He falls for the dummy drop and commits his weight into following up with an elbow to my back as I drop. At the last moment I yank my body back at an impossible angle to avoid his elbow, raising my knee at the same time so that my whole body weight pulls back to meet his exposed face. We both fall to the floor, but only one of us is conscious.

With the rifle I put two bullets in the radio.

A small stack of papers, charts, coded messages and maps lays on the desk. I grab what I can and shove it inside my shirt. I leave the week-old newspaper with the picture of Gerard Rubekki on the front page on the table, push open the door and slip out and around the back of the hut.

Less than 40 seconds it has taken to complete objective 2, but I have not escaped unnoticed.

"Mzungu!" is the repeated shout throughout the camp as fingers point and gunfire is redirected to my pale frame firing back searching for cover.

Objective 3 has now become a little more difficult. The second hut is no longer guarded by two soldiers, instead five or six are firing from its corners and using it as cover as I fall back into spider mode again trying to avoid the stamping foot and swat of bullets.

Disoriented I fall into a shallow ditch used by some of the men as a latrine. I recognise the damp squelch and smell too late as I slide into the low trench, knowing it is the least of my worries. I can't afford to get pinned down here. I raise the rifle and take out as many of their bravest front men as I can. I kill only one but manage to clip three more before my ammo runs out.

My only weapon left is the sidearm. I haven't had time enough to examine it closely to know the model nor the number in the clip. Time isn't on my side. Seeing some of the soldiers have cowered back I make a dash for the flat wall of the second hut, random gunfire flies passed me. I wait for someone to be brave enough to stick his head around the corner then clump him with my fist, take his weapon and shoot him dead.

Armed again I look for those I've already shot, but to my surprise they are already back on their feet and advancing, I note each one has that glazed over look. Three are closing in, firing haphazardly with appalling coordination. I take aim at their chests. They go down. Then they start getting back up again.

I unload the remaining bullets of the AK47 into the three men. Soundlessly they flinch back, fall, then appear to get back up again.

I pull the handgun free of my belt and take aim at their heads. They drop and stay down. A fourth man turns the corner. He too has a milky glaze and is dressed like a villager. I figure they are sending them in like pawns, willing to sacrifice them. Reluctantly I shoot him in the head. It was my last bullet.

My only way into the hut is through the wall. It is my only option; to stay outside is to face a firing squad.

Frantically I kick and pull at the planks that form the side wall. It isn't designed by any chief architect nor was it constructed by a master builder. Fortunately the panels come away easily and I force myself inside, hoping that anyone who had been inside has already come out for the fight. They had, but that meant more men now firing at me outside. I feel a sharp pain in my left arm as I push through the slats: I've been hit. Then the firing stops.

Looking around the inside of the hut I realise why the sudden deathly silence. In the back of my mind I had known it, I'd seen them loading the delivery in here earlier. This is their temporary armory.

I waste no time in arming myself to the teeth.

Through the open broken slats I can see a handful of dark skinned men with pale eyes filling the ditch I had slid into. If they are abhorred by the stench then they make no reaction to it. For my part I can still smell it as it burns my taste buds and singes the hairs in my nostrils.

One soldier seems to be organising the others, no doubt ensuring the hut is surrounded. With enough men they can storm my hideout and shred me with enough bullets to tear me in two. Their only hesitation is in deciding whether I am worth the loss of troops and how many would fall in the process.

Looking around I can see a couple of long wooden caskets filled with AK47's which stick out from where they have been haphazardly thrown in. A couple of smaller boxes lay with the lids off. I recognise the square shape; these don't contain guns but grenades. A third type of box lays on the floor, there are four of them stacked against the side. I take a guess at what is inside as I prize one open with the knife. My guess proves correct: each one contains an RPG-7 and four-pointed cylinder-shaped anti-tank grenades lying in a grey foam casing. I have more than enough to take out every man outside the room - if I can avoid dying first.

A flak jacket with multiple pockets and straps lays on a desk. I put it on. I consider picking up the machete sat next to it but decide I only have hands for one blade. I load the pockets with fully stocked magazines for the assault rifles and pick up two Browning Hi-Power semi-automatic handguns, checking the clips are fully loaded with thirteen bullets per clip, I pick up a few extras to fill any remaining pockets.

Having strapped two fully loaded AK47's across my shoulders - they hurt like hell as they rub against my bleeding arm - I block out the pain as best I can as I wonder whether the hand grenades I've clipped to the hanging rings of the vest are overkill. Catching a glimpse of more movement outside I figure not and lift the RPG from the box, load it, lift out another, and load that one too. I position myself in the centre of the room, satisfied there is no intel to be obtained here but assured that this outfit was well and truly resourced and well financed - I doubt the hut will survive the battle.

I wonder briefly whether sandwiching myself between the two grenade launchers is such a good idea. I would have to time the recoil from both carefully, firing one quickly and then the other, not caring too much for aim. If I judge it wrong I'll rip myself apart as they fire, not to mention risking bursting my own eardrums. It is little compromise to the alternative, which is certain death.

I hope, even if I don't manage to hit anyone, that it will be enough of a distraction to allow me a chance to flee the hut.

I lean back, fire one of the RPG's through the broken slats I'd entered by, slap a hand to my ear in pain, then reach down and fire the other through the door.

Deaf, I run through the busted door before the hot casing of the second launcher has even hit the ground. As I'd hoped, the soldiers on that side have ducked for cover leaving me to open fire as the grenade explodes around them. The grenade takes out a couple. I take out a couple more. Bullets rain at the hut from all directions as most fail to notice I am no longer in there.

Objective 3 achieved.

I run towards the vehicles firing indiscriminately. Being momentarily deaf I am unable to judge the direction of enemy fire or any shouts screamed at me. I take out the men by the trucks easily enough and then use the trucks for cover as I turn and start aiming at any target that moves.

I feel sorry for the villagers, somehow they have been coerced into this, but it is them or me - I have no choice but to gun them down.

Looking back, I am stunned to see one or two wounded men climbing out of a ditch with limbs hanging off like zombies, showing no emotion but still trying to shoot in my direction. The sight almost stops me from pulling the trigger - almost.

I keep shooting until I sense the last of the regular rebels have pulled back and their cannon fodder have fallen permanently. Only then do I climb to the second truck hidden behind the first, which now has too many holes in it to be reliably roadworthy. The keys for the second truck are in the ignition. I turn them. It starts first time. It has more than half a tank, enough to get me to the town Joshua had spoken of. I gun the pedal and tear onto the dirt track hoping not to have to stop for anyone or anything.

<h1 style="text-align:center">5</h1>

An hour later and I am easing off the gas. I have taken a circular route to where I think the town is. There are maps, I suspect, tucked within the crumpled papers lining my chest where they still lay beneath my shirt, but I haven't dared stop to look, and I don't want to be distracted by what I might find on those pages.

I have seen little traffic on the road. One or two cars have passed going in the other direction, looking innocent enough, farmers most probably on their way out to fields beyond the tree line accessed by hidden service roads. A few motorbikes heavy laden with produce or tools of the trade, balanced precariously in a manner that would most certainly have them pulled to the side by the law enforcement of any sensible Western culture. Some of these bikes serve as taxis for as many men as the frame can carry, and in some cases whole family units ride casually on the back with babies in a loose sling at the rear. But most of the traffic has been a steady footfall of pedestrians waking to the day and making their way from secluded abodes in the woods: women making their way into town with heavy bundles and caskets balanced on their heads, their strong necks and backs ensuring their charge never falls to topple onto the infant strapped riding the cushion of butt cheek; children walk barefoot, not to school but to the watering hole or community hand pump, with as many yellow canisters as they can carry, strong muscles bulging from their arms as they haul the weight home. It is all a very typical sight, one I am familiar with, one I love to see, a sight completely ignorant of the turmoil and conflict that engages around them. Sure they know about it, but they are helpless to do anything but live their normal lives knowing the threat of it is always at their door.

I follow the main line of traffic that I see curving round in the direction I had hoped the town was in. As the footfall grows heavier, and the cars more populace, and the dirt road begins to widen I know

I am getting close to a main town. I find a place to ditch the truck: an old abandoned brick building, its construction having never been completed, its walls just high enough to hide the vehicle. Many buildings like this lay scattered on the outskirts of towns; adventurous projects with start-up funds but not enough to complete the task, and so are left unfinished awaiting a time when money will allow the owners to finish the job. The truck will be found eventually, but not until I am well clear of the area.

I climb out and check the back of the truck, it is empty save for the odd discarded boot and lace and empty duffle bag. Most of the soldiers would untie the laces, not knowing how to do them up they would walk with the boots loose and kick them off when being driven about. The bag I could use.

I climb back in the cab and fill the bag with the weapons I still have. I don't want to walk into town parading what I carry, but at the same time I don't want them just lying about for someone to find and misuse.

I pull out the papers from under my shirt and briefly look at what they are. As expected, there are maps and coded messages written in Swahili. Documents and letters about a building project across the mountains by a great lake that is left unidentified. Most disturbing are drawings pertaining to an instruction chart enacting what appears to be some sort of ritual. I've never seen the likes of it before locally, but it looks to be some sort of tribal witchcraft common in remote areas.

Knowing I have little time to find and rejoin Joshua I stash the papers back under my shirt, figuring that would be the safest place for them. I will study them properly later.

The truck's original driver was kind enough to leave behind his jacket, it is an old grey-green military tunic which thankfully is absent of any emblems. It will cover my bloody arm, which now hurts like hell, especially when I throw the strap of the bag over my shoulder, which sets it off bleeding again.

I figure I have little chance of finding Joshua by walking into town and asking people, so am counting on him finding me. Mzungu walking down main street is sure to draw attention and word will soon get round. That will work in my favour for reuniting with my friend but will also shorten the time we could afford to hang around the area.

I leave the cover of the abandoned brick building and join the locals walking towards town, curious but friendly smiling faces greeting me as I walk alongside them.

I've been walking for a while, attracting the expected cursory looks: smiling women, curious boys, wary men. A man eventually draws alongside me as I walk along the main street, which consists of a handful of wooden stalls and one room homes that double as shop fronts. There is a convenience store that sells the national newspaper and confectionaries consistent with such a shop, only the range of choice is much smaller than you'd expect to find in a bigger town or city. A number of hovels hang a curtain over the doorway with a one word sign painted above: 'hotel' read a couple, 'bed' reads another, but a few are much more explicit simply stating 'women'.

Many of the men sit by the curbside, a vacant expression on their faces as they squat in a natural pose that I, and any other westerner, would find uncomfortable. Alcohol or khatt, or even cannabis grown locally, the cause of their stupor as lack of employment and entertainment leaves them reliant on the women to run the home, raise the children, and bring in the income that has forced many a wife and daughter to sell herself to provide that which the men aren't capable of or willing to do. This isn't the case for all, many are hardworking family men, but those at the bottom end, literally the gutter level, sit in their place without trying to hide their shame. It is the effect of years of war and deprivation and a government that doesn't care but ensures any donated aid is creamed off to luxury official compounds and military arms.

The man by my side wears a dirty red vest, long grey shorts, and sandals. His head is shaved and he chews on a piece of grass as he saunters jovially alongside me. We walk two dozen paces together before he speaks.

"Mzungu, you are the aid worker?"

I nod.

"Come with me."

He walks off across the street. I follow, hoping he is friendly but prepared if he is foe.

He seems to want to make small talk, I let him babble without replying, thankful that my hearing is still a bit muffled.

"I've heard of you. You and your wife. You run that aid centre. You gave my aunt and cousin medicine when they had malaria. You've got friends here, and in many places. Sorry about your wife. Joshua told me what happened. You see these people," he says pointing to a group of men sat on the curbside, "they have no hope: no jobs, no money, no care system, and years of war. You know of war? You're pretty handy for an aid worker, were you a soldier before?"

I give him a look that says look away and stop talking, but he doesn't see it, he is looking across the street to an alleyway between two solid brick buildings.

"We're here," he says leading me down the alley to the back of the building. My hand is on the hilt of the blade ready to pull it from my trousers. This is a perfect place for an ambush.

We walk through a series of twists and turns as we navigate the closely packed hovels that house some of the town's residents. I am alert for each turn, each new face that presents itself. Eventually we come to a large unlit room with a man guarding the entrance and another guarding the open doorway to the rear. Joshua rises from his seat on the floor to greet me.

Seeing his smiling face I take my hand off the knife and drop the duffle bag to the floor and embrace my friend with a big hug. One of the other men from the party we had liberated back at the camp earlier is with him, I couldn't see his face initially in the gloom of the room, it is John; that makes sense, with his brother gone he has nothing but shame to return to. He greets me with a thankful handshake, not wanting to let go of my hand. Eventually prizing it away Joshua explains that the others were keen to make haste back to their villages. I nod my understanding; I know their loss and confusion, but at the same time I know nothing is to be achieved by returning; our families are gone, taken, and I for one wasn't going to just give up and allow my son to be abused by rebels.

At Joshua's bidding the other men in the group stand and step forward, some are armed, some wear uniform.

A small band of regular army scouts were camped out in the town seeking intel on the rebel group. They didn't want to return to their garrison empty handed - many in the national army feel the pain of those they are assigned to protect. Too many wars in recent years have created an untrustworthy state with rebel groups vying for power using fear tactics against the people. The poor are marginalised and the rich hated, but none so much as those wearing uniform - any uniform. For many of those who wear it with pride they wish to earn back the people's respect and trust by first eradicating the rebel groups. Many believe the army is the only way to stabilise the nation and overthrow the dictatorship that has fallen into bed with a wealthy Western culture that seems intent on buying up the land - not that anyone ever dares to speak this aloud.

I'd seen it all before, played out in other places. Foreign forces brought in to sway the balance of power to the highest bidder. No matter what the people wanted, ultimately it would come down to the will of whomsoever had the biggest purse.

I greet the soldiers. They are keen to hear what I have to tell of my raid on the camp. I observe their curious worried exchanges as I tell of the white eyes of the villagers, then amazed disbelief of my tale of their weapons cache (only when they open the duffle bag do they concede the truth) and then I earn their respect when I tell of my escape.

They break away from me to conflab together about my tale and what they should do next, leaving Joshua and I alone.

"I'm going to join them. They are the best chance I have of finding my family."

"Can we trust them?" I ask.

"Yes, I believe so."

Their leader, a young man in his early twenties, steps back towards us.

"Come with us," he says.

I stand looking directly in his eyes trying to judge his character.

"Come, join us," he says again. He has pleading in his eyes. They are desperately fighting a losing battle and are in need of a breakthrough.

I give a slow and steady nod.

"How far is your camp?" I ask.

"Two-hour trek south of the mountain," he replies.

"Then we'd better get moving, I have more information to share with your commanding officer." I pat my chest, enough for them to see I am harbouring a stash of papers. They have the manpower and resources I need, and hopefully a medic to patch up my arm, but I'm not going to share my intel with just anyone, and I have no intention of being left on the sidelines when it comes to looking for Benjamin.

6

Captain Akuba was the commanding officer of the regiment this band of scouts were attached to. I never caught his first name as our acquaintance was brief. Having cast to memory as much of the papers as possible and having drawn a rough sketch of two of the maps using paper borrowed from the small van we transported in for the two hour drive to the army camp, Akuba relieved me of my prize.

This camp had no need to be hidden, nor was it in fear of attack. This was an official outpost: well-stocked, well-armed, and well-manned. To attack it would be to instigate a heavy presence retaliation with the potential to spark yet another localised civil war. Too many tribes had already been fractured or decimated by years of fighting and so the nation's tribal kings had no desire to race into yet another unnecessary battle. So long as you were inside the military compound you were safe.

Reluctantly I handed over the papers to Akuba's charge to be inspected and acted upon. He saw immediately the value of what I carried. Some of the papers related to exploratory oil drills in the mountains, some were authorised with proper permits, others shouldn't have been there at all. One letter from a rebel commander signing his name as Commander Jok, was addressed to a tribal leader across the mountain range, in which he promised to do all he could to repel the advance of Western development and disturbance of their native and sacred homeland for the fee of a small piece of land as donation for the use of his troops and their cause. Other papers sighted the advance plans of Gerard Rubekki's oil empire into the wilderness. There were negative calculations as to the potential loss of natural habitat and gainful employment in the region should the explorations for oil prove fruitful. But that was only one side of the story, the papers would appear to have been stolen or copied by a company insider who had mirrored the negative impact statement with a contrived positive one created as a PR exercise. None of this was surprising to me, and in truth it was hard to tell which side of the argument was authentic: Rubekki certainly sold his intent to protect the natives and their habitat well and was seen as a global campaigner for the restoration and regeneration of mined and excavated resource areas. But even the truth of that would fall on the skeptical ears of local tribes ignorant of Western exploits and used to being bullied and manipulated by selfish and sadistic warlords trying to take advantage of the situation in a land and power grab.

The most disturbing of the papers were a series of drawings. They were primitive of the type I'd seen drawn in dirt and sand by Sangomas, local medicine men or witchdoctors. Incantations and rituals depicted in coarse diagrams that made no sense without the explanation of those who had drawn them. I guessed this explained the hold over some of the villagers I had seen and the strange obedience with which they walked eyes blind to the world around them. This was a powerful and dangerous weapon and the rebels had found a way to master it and exploit it.

As for the maps, they were perhaps the most useful intel of all. One was a wide printed map of the country torn from a book, it had a single red circle drawn on it denoting the imminent mountain region which spanned approximately a two hundred mile radius in all directions. Another map was smaller and had marked the local towns and larger groups of dwellings not usually found on a tourist map and covered an area of approximately a fifty mile radius of our current position. The third was of the same area marked only with a large number of simple red crosses sparsely separated. I recognised one - the camp where we had been held. It didn't take a genius to figure out what the other crosses denoted.

In my copy I had been careful to overlay the two smaller maps - I would need these if Akuba decided to exclude me from his offensive.

Joshua and John once again vouched for my usefulness, as if the intel I had provided wasn't enough of a letter of recommendation. Captain Akuba thoughtfully considered where I could be useful in his campaign, questioning me on my military background and knowledge of the country. I gave him very little in this regard: yes, I'd been a soldier, many years ago, and I'd spent a great deal of time in Africa, both in combat and as an aid worker - beyond this my words were few.

He sent me away. 'Go, get refreshed. Wash and eat," he said. And so, dismissed, I went off and tried to busy myself with a meal and a shower. It was good to wash the mud and grime from my body, along with the remnants of Jenny's blood which still crusted around the edges of my hairline. I wondered at the state I had looked as I walked into the town to meet Joshua and what the locals must have made of me. I tried hard to cast away the image of Jenny's pleading eyes staring up at me from her severed head in my lap as her blood washed away across my body.

At the mess hall I was brought some fresh fatigues from the store to replace my torn and bloodied clothes. Only then did I admit to my wound and request a medic to patch me up. I wanted the pain of having the bullet dug out and a needle sowing me up. All these things I needed as a distraction.

Whilst Akuba contemplated my fate, I realised that for the first time I had no direction, no motivation of action I could take to block out from my mind that which chased down my shadow fleeing from the sun.

Jenny flushed my vision in multi-coloured high definition, kneeling on the floor, her eyes pleading, having been raped and tortured, with *him* waving that gun in her face.

I tried to force the image out as I went through the blur of motions of mindless activities, my mind and body numb to the grief that threatened to overshadow me. And it wasn't just me. Outside I saw Joshua sat on the floor sobbing, his head in his hands. Elsewhere John too was weeping the loss of his brother Moses. We all had our grief. We all had our loss.

I went to Joshua and knelt down by him.

"We'll find her, Joshua. We'll get your daughter back," I promised him. It was a promise I had no right to speak, I couldn't ensure I'd be able to deliver on it, but my words were of a determination that he knew I meant, and I could see in his eyes that he trusted in my resolve to restore what was lost or else deliver hell trying.

Akuba sent a man to fetch us. We three, myself, Joshua and John, went to his office. There were pictures on the wall behind his desk of various rebel soldiers, snapshots taken over a period of time at various towns and compounds about the countryside. The most prominent figure was a brute of a man, a scar across his face - it was him.

Akuba pointed to one of the pictures of the man that had killed Jenny. "This is Daniel Jok. He is the head. Cut it off and they all fall. He is the driving force. The problem I have had is that I can't find him. Then you walk in with these." He flung the maps across the desk. "Join us. Help us. I want to put a strike force together to go out and attack these outposts."

"Who will lead?" I asked.

"My men."

I nodded. "We have different priorities."

"Of course. You have children to find. This I think would be the best way for us all to find what we are looking for. I have little resources or men to spare so you add to my numbers, but if anyone asks, you don't work for me. This is not a government sanctioned offensive you understand. They don't see what is happening here, or they choose to ignore it. My eyes are open. I want these rebels caught and our wives and children returned."

His words were sincere. I didn't need to deliberate much on the subject as I found my head nodding in agreement.

And so began our journey, our tornado of terror that we would unleash upon the rebels as we used their own maps against them.

Of course, not everything was plain sailing.

7

Three months of raiding parties has taken its toll. We are physically and emotionally drained. It's hard to explain the exhilaration of bursting through the camouflage of woodland cover to assault an unknown and potentially explosive ground force.

It has been a long time since I've had to endure the hardships of a military exercise; staying away from base and living off limited supplies, rationing every bean and every bullet. You get to know your team pretty well under these circumstances. You learn who is strong and who is weak, and who to trust to cover your back. Akuba's men are on the whole a good bunch, honest men wanting to make a difference in their nation, fighting for a cause not just for a job. Our team is small, and occasionally we get reinforcements or replacements when we stop at staging posts, usually small towns where a rendezvous has been arranged. Mostly we have a core team of about ten men under the command of Lotu, a thirtysomething career soldier, not an officer, but an infantry footman respected and trusted enough by Akuba to run the operation. An officer has to be accounted for, Lotu doesn't. I get the impression this isn't his first rodeo on such a mission.

Lotu, it transpired as we sat one night around the campfire trading stories, had been a school teacher in the north of the country when civil war with another set of guerillas long defeated burned down the school and shot the principal dead in front of the kids. Lotu considered himself lucky to have survived but knew he couldn't go back to teaching the children knowing the trauma they had gone through and may have to face again. And so he joined the army, vowing to rid his people of this seemingly endless plague of terror.

Lotu asked about my background and my experience. I fought for my country, I had told him, and I had fought without them, then a woman changed my life and showed me a better way. I said no more

46

than this and Lotu and the others accepted it in sight of my loss, though I knew they were desperate to know more.

Our maps have proved true, if not detailed enough. The marked crosses are, as expected, enemy camps, but not all are manned. Some are small arms supplies and temporary bases, dugouts in the woods to act as shelter and staging posts for soldiers moving on elsewhere. Some are food supplies. Others still contained animals, poached game, some dead, some caged and alive. We found a haul of elephant tusks unconvincingly buried at one site. This, we assumed, is how they finance some of their operations, by hunting and capturing animals for illegal sales overseas. We already knew that there was a large train of ivory transported via pirate routes to China. National Park wardens had been warning of the dwindling numbers due to poaching for years and everyone knew rebel forces were responsible for the bulk of it.

These weren't the finds that interested me. The ones where we found people were what got me excited. If it was just rebel soldiers I learned quickly to relish disposing of them and torturing them for information - that gave us more crosses to mark on our map. If it was women or children or villagers then I welled with relief at being able to free them, but the horror of what they had endured fueled my hate for Jok and his men and made me fearful for the children we hadn't yet found.

8

We lost John the same day we found Joshua's daughter. It was a bittersweet day.

I say we lost him, he didn't die straightaway, the wound festered for three days of agonising fever as the infection spread from the rusty knife that had pierced his abdomen, the sickness sweating through his pores before we could get him to a medic. By then it was too late and he slipped away before we could safely reach civilization.

We lost many men this way, usually the fearful and untrained.

I feared Joshua would fall to the same fate as he spiraled into a cocoon of self-loathing after his little girl's body was found in amongst the abused and discarded corpses in an open pit used as a grave. I hoped he would turn his hatred back on those that had caused this atrocity.

The camp we raided that day was a harem for the rebels. How many men had wandered through and satisfied their selfish desires on these women and young girls was anyone's guess. Tearful, the surviving women were led out to safety and transported to a rehabilitation centre south of the mountain which was set up by a Canadian charity.

The grave we found was filled with those girls and women who had proved physically unappealing or who had refused to serve their new masters in such a way, or who had simply cracked emotionally, their bodies and minds broken.

Joshua's daughter, I remembered her from the village as a spritely, joyful young thing, always dancing and eager to help the mothers with chores. She lay crumpled, eyes wide and lifeless, her lips severed, the soft tissue of her nose missing and her ears sliced away. She had suffered. She still wore the dress she wore the day she was taken - the day Benjamin was taken. If it wasn't for the dress we may have passed her over.

Joshua collapsed there and then. He wept tears of joy that he had found her and that her suffering was over, but his heart was wrenched out to the point that I feared he would not recover to draw breath.

Men littered the camp. Those caught with their pants down had fallen as easy targets. In our enthusiasm to enact justice we were blind to an advancing patrol to our rear. It was they who gunned down our rear guard and pinned down our defences. So close were they that we were forced to engage at close quarters. Swords were drawn, machetes and daggers - and so fell John.

It was our worst defeat and it forced us to regroup and reassess our options.

I said it was a bitter sweet day; yes our losses were great, but for me - and you can call me callous if you wish - it was a day that secured me command, as Akuba finally, via a radio communication, submitted to my superior planning and experience above that of his own men, sending word for me to lead the unit in light of having lost his own commanders in the fight. Lotu wasn't dead, but the injuries he received in that attack would see him benched for a month at least. I'd be happy to serve under him again if he was to return, but at that moment time was pressing and Akuba knew the worth of keeping the pressure on and persisting with the mission. Besides, I wanted to do things my way and step things up a gear.

That day also secured me Joshua. He had become a formidable foot soldier in his desperation to find his daughter, but now she was dead he was no longer conflicted in his emotions and fears. In fact, fear was gone and rage now consumed him. Once the grief sickness wore off some days later, Joshua confirmed his wish to remain as my second in command with a determination to wipe out every last rebel he could find.

9

One thing I had noticed as we tore through camp after camp was the lack of controlled villagers the farther from the mountain we got, as though the mountain itself played a part in their trance. They had been absent from the women's camp, presumably not needed for the games played there. But where we noticed them more was where we encountered the boys: blind lone soldiers standing post, or in twos or threes randomly scouting out a tree line. It was as if their young minds were more susceptible to whatever hold this powerful spell held over them.

I feared for Benjamin. These boys didn't react to us with kindness or welcome us as saviours, instead they fired at us. Knowing them to be children, innocent victims, we didn't fire back, not to kill them anyway. And so they were never rescued, having run back into the forest to seek the safety of their new masters.

If I ever found Jok, and I had every intention of doing so, I had in mind to slowly cut his head from his shoulders for all that he had done, not just to me but to these people I had come to care about.

10

I have lost track of time since I was taken. I have been resisting all their attempts to turn me, as they have done so many others, but now my will is waning.

My body is weak. My mind is distraught. My senses have been terrorised and tortured, yet still I hold out a mustard seed of hope that my father will save me.

The rumours of 'The Mzungu Warrior' have reached us even hear. We hear the soldiers talking about it, how their camps are being raided by the central army and how their commander is a Western aid worker turned killing machine.

There is fear and embarrassment amongst the guerillas. They are being beaten back by an untrained white man, a charity worker. I figure this is why I'm not beaten as severely as the others, and why Commander Jok has instructed that I be protected and not killed. I can be used as leverage when it comes to it.

They know it is me that drives my *Mzungu baba,* my white father, to fight. They have a picture of us together with my adopted mother, Jennifer. It used to be up in the medical hut where she worked in the village, Jok must have taken it from there. He quizzes me on my relationship with baba, always with a hint of malice in his eyes as he speaks. He seems to know of my baba but won't speak to me of how.

Commander Jok keeps a close eye on me, visiting the compound regularly and trying to persuade me to join his cause. He says I will be converted eventually, one way or another.

I have lost many of my friends from the village. They patrol the woods as senseless soldiers, raping and pillaging with no emotion nor fear of consequence, their conscience corrupted and destroyed. Few are here with me now.

There is a sickness amongst some of the boys that affects their eyes. They look blind but they can see. They look absent but are aware of their surroundings. They look alive but act as if dead. Sometimes boys leave well but fearful and return sick and strangely obedient to the will of the guards.

I do not want to catch this sickness.

11

Finally, we have a break. Jok has been sighted near a village that has been raided not twenty miles from our position. A road cuts through the low-lying hills in-between, meaning if we are quick we have a chance of catching him.

We radioed in our location and objective. It was met with approval from Captain Akuba who replied agreeing to send extra troops in support. They'll be up to three hours behind us. Air support is unavailable; the squadron's two helicopters have been seconded to the capital city to help with the security arrangements to protect the foreign nationals flying in for the UN Sustainable Development Summit being held there. Many big business representatives and politicians would be present and those who resided or had interests in our little Central African nation would be keen to hush up the ongoing troubles outside of the main capital arena. Whatever minimal military or diplomatic resources available would be used to the maximum to show a greater force and strength for the nation than was actually in place.

We had heard rumours of villages in the area being attacked which was why we had moved our campaign to this section on our map. Children and women were still being taken, villagers were still being killed and homes burned. It sickens me.

There is no enemy camp marked on our map close to where the reports are coming in so I suspect, in line with the news that Jok himself is present, that maybe his local base of operations is situated here, and for that reason it has been omitted from the map due to its importance. If this is true then I have high hopes that not only will we find Jok, but also Benjamin. What is between us is personal and I know he will use Benjamin to get to me.

We travelled seventeen miles and then left our drivers on the road holding back until called for. They are our rear guard. We need to approach stealthily through the forest, fanning out, searching for the camp we suspect is there but have no definite coordinates for. The likelihood is we will stumble across it and draw fire, but I hope we have a chance of observing before our assault to give us enough time to plan our attack. Too many civilians and good soldiers have been lost in rash unplanned raids - I don't want this one going wrong - too much is at stake.

I lead one team to the right of the road. Joshua leads another to the left. Flanking the one road we hope between us to encounter something worthy of intelligence before we strike our target. We keep radio contact to a minimum, a series of clicks and squarks we understand to be non-verbal signals which unwanted listening ears shouldn't understand.

We had heard earlier the rumble of trucks and smaller vehicles travelling in convoy along the road in the distance, travelling away from us in the other direction. The road stretches for another thirty miles following the river south from the mountain. I hope this means the bulk of their troops are on the move, I'm not interested in them. I just hope Jok and Benjamin aren't on the departing transports.

As we draw close to the camp there is an eerie silence over the prevailing forest - that is how we know we are almost on top of it. The birds know. The insects know. The primates know. Every creature that crawls or slivers under the canopy of the trees seems to sense the evil that is hiding in the forest. Darker than Mirkwood it feels, with more dangers than giant spiders hiding ready to pounce. I'm sure even the hobbits felt taller and more confident than we do slowly creeping through, our fingers twitching at every shadow and crack of a branch.

My radio squelches twice. Joshua has visual contact.

Moments later gunfire erupts in the distance on the far side of the road. Joshua has engaged with the enemy.

From what we can hear they are ahead of us on the left of the road. We need to get across, flank the enemy. I am about to give the signal when I stop and crouch low. My men follow suit. Something has spooked me. I'm not sure what. Then I see it. A trembling green that doesn't flutter with the wind, of which there is none, but instead shakes with fear and uncertainty.

I can see the barrel of a rifle. Then another.

They are scouts or sentries. The more I stare the more their features come into focus and distinguish themselves from the surrounding foliage. They are young men, probably not even out of their teens, probably former child soldiers now left with the charge of protecting the camp.

The gunfire dies down. There is a click and a squelch on my radio. Joshua's troops are victorious, but they haven't found the camp.

Instinct tell me I am on the right side of the road and that these sentinels aren't attacking because they are hoping we will leave to cross the road and bypass what they are guarding.

The fact that they haven't opened fire tells me they are few in numbers, it could even be that the two I can see are all that is left behind to guard the outer perimeter on this side of the road. I think about the gunfire I'd heard: short sporadic bursts, little return fire.

I signal Joshua with a double squelch of my radio, then give a gesture with my hand to instruct my men to take cover behind the trees. Crouching low in a sudden movement I take aim and fire at the nearest combatant.

I see a spray of blood spoil his camouflage as he falls backwards. The second hiding figure gives away his position with a short orange flare from the mussel of his weapon before he retreats into the bushes before the return fire can tear him in two.

I allow my men to loosen their nerves with a fifteen second open range on the forest ahead before I signal the ceasefire.

If he has survived his run for cover the second guard could have met with reinforcements farther back. If not, he would be lying bleeding not far from his post. My guess is he has made a dash for the cover of the camp and I am eager to follow the trail he would have left behind as he ran.

We advance quickly to where they had stood. The first man is laying dead where I expected him to be. A trail of blood limps back from the other side of the tree. We follow it to find a second figure in his death throes. He expires as we crouch to him, sparing me the trouble of having to put a bullet in his head.

Another blood trail leads yet farther away from us - there had been three of them at least.

I crouch defensively. My men do the same.

The sounds of the forest breathe loudly as we hold our breath listening for the sudden creak of its bones as it moves to accommodate the bacteria, the cancer trying hide from our medicine.

Then suddenly there is a running and stamping and shouts from both sides as two assailants, surely knowing the attack to be futile, attempt to confuse us by breaking for cover and launching at us from different directions at the same time.

We are too used to this amateur ambush tactic. We are in a low arrow formation as we advance, each of my men picking a point ahead of them and firing indiscriminately at anything that moves. It could have been elephants charging at us and the result would have been the same. The front side of the trees and the men that leapt from behind them were riddled with holes beyond count.

As the smoke settles one of my men whispers my name and points to the tree canopy. I look to where his finger indicates. There, just between the stag head branches of two trees is a wooden turret - a lookout post rising above the camp.

Binoculars are passed along the line as the other men secure our location and signal to Joshua that we have found the prize. He will circle round and approach from the side, careful not to draw our line of fire - last thing we want is to shoot our own.

One figure stands in the tower, a boy no more than fifteen, his body and head still giving no indication that he is alerted by the shooting, though he must have been. His eyes are pale and unseeing so that it is impossible to gage where he's looking.

"Children in the camp," I say to the men. There is an audible groan. They all know what it means: 'blind boys' as we have come to call them - child soldiers under a spell. None of us want to shoot them.

We draw closer, using the trees for cover until we come to a clearing. A wide bank of trees have been hewn down and carved into spikes pointing outward protecting a mesh fence around a dozen or so sturdy wooden buildings. It is clearly constructed as a permanent settlement and is likely well used. My hopes that this is their main base in the region are bolstered.

I take stock of the camp, my great hopes for it fading the more I look as I bide for time for Joshua to get into position.

My first concern is the lack of adults. With the exception of the men in the forest that we had killed I can see only four men guarding the camp: two at the front gates and two at the rear. A few children aged about ten or twelve meander about in a zombie-like trance. The children don't appear armed which immediately raises my suspicions. They are trying to lure us in.

The second thing I notice is the lack of vehicles: there aren't any. That means Jok is unlikely to be here. It also means that there is no escape plan for anyone in the camp, if they don't defeat us then they expect to die. I hate the suicide fighters, they are the most dangerous and unpredictable - you can never truly second guess a man willing to die for his cause.

My hope is that the huts are empty of soldiers but full of children.

A second turret rises on the far side of the camp but a tree within hides its occupant. Joshua radios in his position, he has a view of the far turret confirming a 'blind boy' is stood guard.

I have a bad feeling about this but know we can't linger much longer, we have to attack.

A full assault, frontal and rear, seems the easiest option. The gates are unchained so all we need to do is storm the four guards, push through to the courtyard beyond and take cover by the nearest huts and wait for their defences to come out of hiding. I hold a couple of men back by the tree line, one of which is in possession of the Russian Dragunov sniper rifle we had liberated from another camp on a previous raid. If we get pinned down then hopefully we will have some cover fire from outside the camp.

We sneak forward and take out the two guards at the front gate easily enough, maybe too easily. We shoot our way through and take cover behind some boxes near the gate house as planned, then proceed to the courtyard and the first of the lager buildings. We don't draw any fire. The sentinels in the lookout towers just stare down at our forked attack stance blankly.

"What are they waiting for?" one of my men questions. I shake my head uncertainly, fearing the worst.

All is still. All is eerily quiet.

We edge forward.

I can see Joshua at the end of the alleyway between the rows of buildings lined up like a prisoner of war camp, both of us moving slowly with caution. In the chasm that separates us, a couple of raggedly dressed boys slow pace as if in a skunk driven dream, their minds in a far away place as their feet follow in a remote-controlled trance. As we watch them they appear harmless, capturing our attention as we draw deeper into the camp.

"Damn it!" I curse myself as I snap into a defensive position, turning my back on the visible children just in time to realise we have walked straight into a trap as the hut doors burst open and the blind boys in full military fatigues start firing at us.

One of my men, who is slow to react to the swift movement, takes a barrage of about twenty shots as he stands the obvious target, twitching and fitting in the air spasmodically so that the boys still think he is a live target that won't go down.

It buys us some time as the rest of us roll under the struts of the huts and fire back from ground level.

I didn't see what happened to Joshua's team, but I expect that he had come under the same ambush.

My fallen man, once he had finally hit the ground, had covered our escape with his body, allowing us to crawl to the far side of the hut without fear of being shot at as we claw the dust, hoping any snakes hiding in the shade have fled at the disturbance.

Pushing my gun forward as I crawl, I glance back to see a darkened shadow squirming like a demonic insect behind me, the only thing giving away its identity being the whites of its eyes that seem to glow with tenebrous ferocity.

I crawl faster, feeling this is more a scene from a horror movie than the fields of battle I am used to. My colleague is slower, whether he is snagged on something or claustrophobia has taken hold in the cramped space I can't tell, but his ankle is caught. The grip of the unseen hand from beneath the bed has reached out to him and has a firm hold. He screams and thrashes with his foot trying to kick off the spectre that's claimed him. He manages to spin his body just enough to reach his rifle back behind him and blindly fire a couple of shots towards his feet as the overwhelming strength of the child begins to pull him backwards. His shot hits its target and the head explodes and the lights of his eyes go dim.

We crawl faster then as other shadows follow suit.

I make it out. My colleague, having found his motivation, rushes out after me still screaming.

We are one man down and stood to the rear of an occupied and hostile threat with the doors to yet more open cabins in front of us. We raise our rifles to the blind boys and start shooting.

It was a blood bath, one that would haunt me for the rest of my life. We massacred so many children that day - not willingly you understand, but out of self-preservation. That was the sick inhuman and grossly barbaric tactics of the man we faced. Jok knew if he couldn't destroy us physically then he would destroy us mentally.

Half my men perished that day. It would have been worse if it wasn't for our snipers covering us from the trees. And of the rest of us none, including myself and Joshua, ever raided another village again.

Madly and without any order or discipline we ran through the camp, taking cover where we could, disarming children where we could, and shooting them when we had to. We shot to injure not to kill, but not everyone was as good a shot as me.

I suspected most of the captured children were held in this one camp, and my suspicions were confirmed when we burst into the last hut.

"Wazimu Mbwa si hapa! Wazimu Mbwa si hapa!" the boy in the front of the small gaggle starts shouting, the others behind him echoing in chorus as they all open fire with vicious grimacing faces.

It is a shout we have heard many times before as we went from camp to camp and small outpost to outpost. Scared men cried it as they surrendered their weapons, hoping it would earn them leniency. Blind boys and men alike would shout it as if programmed, little emotion carrying on their words as they followed a hidden command buried deep in their subconscious. None, however, had ever shouted it with the vehemence of these boys intent on gunning us down.

"Wazimu Mbwa si hapa!" They continued to shout in a chant as we dived for cover once again. 'Mad Dog isn't here,' is what it means, that was the name Daniel Jok allows them to call him. That is his guerilla name, the name he uses to instill fear. To those he does business with or wants to be respectable to he is Commander Jok, but to everyone else he is Mad Dog.

Mad Dog had set these boys up to kill or be killed, only one he knew I wouldn't pull the trigger on, and he was stood before me now trying to kill me - Benjamin.

One by one their ammunition fails, expires as it had done in all the other huts we'd burst open once we learnt our lesson on how to approach the problem. The boys all stayed put until they felt a disturbance outside their door and then they went on the attack. Once we learned their programming, we knew all we had to do was trick them into opening the doors and shoot at the walls opposite and at the dead corpses we dragged into view and wait for their bullets to run out.

As the last casings fell, I stepped into view of the boys, my boy at their head - this was how Jok had planned it. Benjamin looking through me with those blind milky eyes, continually pulling on the trigger of his AK47.

I feel a trickle down my cheek as I weep bitterly for my boy, but he doesn't seem to notice as he reaches for the dagger at the rear of his pants and leaps out from the raised doorway. I sidestep his lunge and punch him heavily to the ground. He falls like a sack of potatoes but, like all the other children we had fought, he doesn't stay down. I don't want to shoot him. It might not kill him but it will scar him, and who knows how it will incapacitate him afterwards - not that we have ever cured anyone of the sickness; those we had encountered were either dead or we had let run to avoid killing them.

Benjamin rises to his feet, but it isn't the boy I had once known in the village. His focus is on me as if he seems to know who I am but is looking through someone else's eyes. And then Joshua drops him from behind. He had crept up and buckled his legs at the knees with a simple kick. I follow it up with a smashing punch to the side of the head. It isn't enough to kill him, I guess I was hoping for maybe a reset, either way he is out cold.

12

He came around tied to a tree with a bunch of other kids. We'd bunched them in groups of three or four and roped them to the trunks. We had to knock them all unconscious first and tie them quickly. Even some of the ones we thought were dead suddenly came running, screaming like banshees from where they had fallen trying to tear at us with their nails. We had to keep hitting them to subdue them. We felt sick to the stomach, but there was no alternative. At least two of the boys had their skulls caved in accidentally beyond repair.

Leaning down close to Benjamin I can see no sign of recognition in his blank eyes. No happy smile for his baba. Only the snapping and gnashing of teeth as he senses me near.

I withdraw and assess our situation. We have forty three children and two trucks that can carry ten men each, and in addition we have three jeeps loaded (as the trucks were) top to bottom with supplies: fuel, food, ammunition, shelter. The drivers and their escorts give us another twelve men. Nine of my assault team are still standing, but all are either injured or traumatised; they will make it back to base, but they are running on adrenalin and their tanks are near empty.

As our vehicles drive into the camp entrance and park up in the courtyard I signal the drivers to create a perimeter defence. We will have to hold out here until our expected support arrives; it should be here soon, I hope. One of the drivers signals as he climbs out of the cab that he needs to speak to me, but before I can turn to him Joshua sidles up to me.

"Akuba says two days at least."

"What! Why?"

"The convoy that left here has attacked our garrison to the east. There is a larger force of militia than we have seen before. All resources have been diverted there. Air support is still tied up at the capital."

"Where have they got all these men from?" I don't expect Joshua to answer, it is an outspoken thought as my mind echoes tactics I'd seen before in distant lands. There is more to this than meets the eye, but I can't focus on that now, Benjamin is my main concern.

Joshua nods his head to the injured men. "They're expecting backup to be rolling down the road any minute. I'm not sure these men can hold out here for two days in the state they're in." Joshua is right, they are a fractured and damaged group.

"We have no choice," I reply, "we don't have enough transport to get the kids to safety and we need the trucks here in case we need to leave in a hurry. Raid the huts for weapons and ammo and patch up the wounded. We'll have to hunker down and await evac."

"And if they return before support arrives?"

"Just keep on the radio, ramp up our need for backup." I step away. I share Joshua's concerns, the very real threat that we are sitting ducks along with having the charge of village kids that needed removing to a safe distance from the war zone. We could flee and leave them, but after what we had just been through to save them, abandoning them just wasn't an option.

The driver had walked around to the back of the truck and had been joined by his shotgun passenger and another driver who seemed to have knowledge of what was in the back. The first driver pulls the tarp up as I corner the bumper.

"We found this in the woods near the roadside," says the truck's driver, revealing a scraggly unshaven African sat cross legged mumbling to himself. His eyes are blank, white like the blind boys. He has trinkets in his loosely worn long braided hair, and boned necklaces and bracelets, and his face is adorned in white and red paint.

"He was like this when we found him," says the driver.

His mumble is repetitive. He is chanting. Symbols painted on his arms, legs and torso are familiar, we have seen them many times carved into trees and on the sides of huts we have raided, even here on the doors where the children had been hiding. The white paste I suspect is chalked bone, the red I am certain is blood.

As I stare, the witchdoctor's eyes roll down from where he has been hiding them in his trance, and he grins, then his grin becomes a laugh. He stops abruptly and points at me.

"Nyeupe Mpiganaji," he says with a hint of both fear and mocking. It means 'white warrior' in his tongue and I know immediately he'd been left behind on purpose for me to find.

13

My first instinct is to shoot him dead there and then in the back of the truck. My men must have seen the grimace of hatred on my face as they quickly intervene.

"He is not responsible for this," says one, the shotgun passenger, Sayed is his names. "He is Inyanga."

I have heard the term before but don't fully understand its meaning. All I understand is that he was a Sangoma, a witchdoctor, and witchcraft was responsible for the hold over my son who seemed intent on killing me.

"He can help us," Sayed insists.

I'm not listening. I don't want to hear. All my hate is being fuelled towards the ragged skin and bones figure sat grinning before me. If I can't get to Jok, the instigator of my pain, then I will take it out on everyone that serves him willingly.

"Inyanga are local Sangoma's," says Koffe, the driver, as if I didn't understand that much. "They are healers. They sell items to villagers to keep them well and heal their ills and injuries."

I half look at him. He has my attention, but I still don't understand what he means.

"He is not the cause of the blindness," says Sayed. "He says he has been following the trail of the curse and marking its path."

Suddenly my mind flashes with an image of this man marking warnings on trees. For the first time I seriously want to know what those carvings mean.

"He has been trying to warn us," Sayed continues. "He says Wazimu Mbwa has employed a powerful Thakathi, a dark witch to curse the people and to give power to him in return for protection of her sacred lands."

My mind quickly realigns my assumptions: Jok has promised to protect the witch's hunting ground from the oil baron's drilling in return for an army he can control, and this *Inyanga* could possibly know of a way to break the spell.

"What does he know?" I ask, resistant of hope. "Can he break the curse?"

Sayed says something to the witchdoctor in Swahili. He flicks his grey dreadlocks back behind him, flings his head back and laughs.

This is hopeless and his antics are causing my blood to boil again. I make to move away before I do something I will regret, but Koffe grabs my arm. "Wait," he says.

I turn back to look. The old man is nodding his head and gesturing for someone to help him to his feet so he can climb out of the back of the truck.

As Koffe and Sayed help him out I try to guess his age. Black men are notorious for being ageless in appearance and I had at first taken this one to be late thirties or early forties. It is hard to judge it due to all the markings and paint on his skin, some markings I observe are cuts, scars from self-inflicted wounds most likely performed in the course of rituals to whatever false gods he worships. Stumbling out unsteadily I can see he is much older, maybe even double the age I had originally suspected, which is unusual within a rural African community to have lived so long. If he attributed his long life to his craft then he undoubtedly would have an abundance of followers.

With his feet planted on solid ground he crouches in the customary manner and uses his finger to draw in the dirt. He doesn't write in words I recognise as either English or Swahili, but instead in some sort of pictograph. Some are symbols I recognise: a sideways cross reported danger; a small letter 'e' sitting on its tail means 'to go around' as in a path or journey; an arch joining to what looks like a dagger with its blade pointing south east means literally 'death bridge'. Don't ask me how I know these things, they are just random pieces of information lodged in the subconscious picked up after too many years living in the wilds.

Other symbols are new to me, but I can see that Sayed at least has some knowledge of the arts being practised. I wonder, not for the first time, just how common these primitive practises are in the villages that I have visited. Had they hidden them from me when I had visited among them? How many of my men knew the symbols we had passed by so many times, and did they not speak up out of fear of the unknown, or the known that they didn't understand and could not control?

My western mind refutes any notion of power or control that this nonsensical hypnosis could have over me, but these people are mostly uneducated and easily manipulated and enchanted.

Sayed begins a rough translation, but he keeps shaking his head, unhappy at the string of words he tries to tie together. I look to the old man to discern any recognition in his face from the translation. I stare beneath the macabre paint on his face, dried and flaked to reveal wrinkled leathery skin, darker in patches than an average African but ashen with age in others. He almost appears two-tone, mostly his right side deeply scorched by the sun as though he has lain like Ezekiel on one side in obedience to his god.

"This one here say stone, this one flower." Sayed points to a series of triangles stood on point looking like cocktail glasses, one empty, two with a level of liquid, and one with a curly straw. "These three are similar, but you see the differences here, no line means water, the single line across is earth, and the one with the squiggle on top means clay. Stone flower, water from the earth in clay jar - maybe?" He shakes his head unconvinced at his own interpretation.

The old man draws another symbol, this one looks like a word I recognise in English, it spells out ANA, only the first A draws a line to the left to give it a foot at the start.

"What does that mean?" I ask.

"The same. Or equal quantity."

"Water and earth in clay jar in equal quantity?" Koffe suggested.

Was it possible it was a shopping list? My hopes rise as the translation begins to sound like a recipe Macbeth's three witches could make use of. I wait to see if eye of newt, and toe of frog, wool of bat, and tongue of dog come into the ingredients. Is it possible this so-called healer knows of a cure for the curse that has captured our children?

"This one," Koffe points to the one that looks like a flattened off see through umbrella that Sayed has translated as stone, "may be something else." He pauses, doubting himself.

"Spit it out, nothing sounds stupid or crazy anymore," I try to reassure him.

"What if stone is mountain?" he asks.

The old man laughs again and points off into the distance. I follow the line of his arm north to the mountain we have been skirting around for the last few months.

"Thakathi's mountain, water, earth and her flower," speaks the old man in all seriousness as though great peril lay upon his words.

"You speak English!" I exclaim in astonishment and mild annoyance. He could have told us all this without the elaborate drawings, but somehow I know he wanted me to figure it out by myself. This was for me, all of it. This was my task. My challenge. My quest.

"If I get you these things, can you break the curse on the boys?"

The old man nods. "I can, but can you?" He gives a toothless grin, daring me to risk everything on a fool's errand to retrieve what he asks for. I don't believe in his faith, despite the effects of the strange magic hold I have witnessed, but here I am contemplating racing off to acquire a potion which requires me to have faith in the words of a senile old man.

I look back at the tree where Benjamin is tied. What else do I have to lose? It isn't as though we have any other leads on how to restore them back to themselves. Even if Jok has laid this as a trap, leaving behind the old man as I had originally suspected, I can't really see an alternative.

I turn on my heels in search of Joshua, barking back an order to unload one of the jeeps and make sure it is fully fueled and with surplus in the back.

Finding Joshua, I tell him of my thoughts. I'm not asking his opinion and he doesn't give it, but I can tell by his expression that he approves and would do the same if his child still lived. I tell him to hold out for reinforcements and instruct him to give me two days - I hope it won't take longer.

Taking one last lingering look at Benjamin as I pass, I make my way towards the jeep.

The old Sangoma grips my arm as I get in. "Beware to trespass on Kyala's grave. Deal with Fumo first. Water and earth and her flower in equal measure."

I don't understand all that he says. I shake my arm free and climb in, knowing the familiar names he mentioned are folklore I have heard but never trusted in but now will have to try and dredge up from my memory banks.

I turn the key and spin the jeep around and head north towards the mountain.

14

Many things cross my mind as I drive at breakneck speed across the main road marked on the map running north toward the mountain. There is little traffic, neither vehicular nor pedestrian, as if an omen has flown ahead of me to warn the people to clear the road for my passage. I fear a collision, a breakdown, a congestion, but my concerns are unwarranted as I thrash the jeeps engine to its limit.

Jok's forces have moved farther south on an offensive against the government's army. This can only mean one thing: he is vying for power not only of the region but of the country as a whole, and for that he needs to control the local forces first. It is an ambitious plan, beyond the ambitions of what I know Daniel Jok to be capable of. I can't help but wonder who is pulling his strings. Jok is a mercenary, has been for years, so who is he working for now?

My problems with Jok are not my main concern right now and thinking about him only fuels my hate which masks the sorrow I feel at Jenny's death. If I dwell too much on him I will collapse in a fit of emotion at the loss of the one person who had held me together and showed me purpose, the one person who had given me a direction to follow away from the violent lifestyle I had been living.

Of course, I was driving on one of the main roads up to the mountain. That great tree covered rock face lying up ahead, visible for miles around. There was no chance of missing my destination and taking a wrong turn, and yet I had no idea where I was going.

What am I supposed to do when I get to the mountain? There is a road going in both directions around its base - I knew neither of these would be right. The map shows two other tracks up, one on this side and one on the farther side. There would be more of course, smaller pathways winding into unmarked settlements of mountain dwellers. There are possibly eco huts set up by researchers, geologists, and wildlife supporters who use the abundant ecology of the region to study and record the natural habitat and the effects of the human condition upon it - that is if Jok's men haven't scared them off, or the likes of Rubekki's oil drilling platforms sampling the land haven't bullied the locals into submission.

What I'm looking for is likely to be off the beaten track. The narrowest road will most likely be the most fruitful. I hope to find someone, a resident of the mountain I can employ as a guide, or at the very least question for information.

From a distance the mountain looks smooth and serene, but I know from experience terrain such as this will be fraught with danger and will harbour a montage of obstacles in the dense fur covering of trees and rocky outcrops and dips that form the gauntlet I will have to climb. I have ropes and the basic of climbing gear in the jeep for when I will have to abandon the wheels, knowing that period on foot will slow me down. Thinking about it forces my right foot to the floor; I haven't given myself enough time to achieve the task. Getting to the mountain, finding this remote Thakathi's temple, or whatever it is, and retrieving ingredients I am still fairly vague on, and then returning before Jok's men try to reclaim his lost blind boys is even more ambitious than anything my adversary is attempting.

I look to the arc of the sun; I have about five hours of daylight left. I floor it to the point that the jeep's wheels lift from the ground, and pray I won't hit any potholes to fly me off course.

15

Cephas isn't much of a talker in spite of the person he is named after. He is sixteen, and untouched and untroubled by the complaints and concerns of the lowlands. The mountain and its connecting range lying to the north seem unperturbed, unaffected, and distinctly removed from the rest of the world around it.

I had found him fishing in a stream that fed into a creek running down the eastern side of the mountain. I had long abandoned the jeep, having taken all the supplies I could carry. All whom I'd stopped to ask the way seemed to point a nervous and uncertain finger in the same direction. Clearly, they weren't used to being asked the way to find the Sangoma that lived on the mountain and were keen for it not to be their business by ensuring I found my way and didn't bother them further. What was Sangoma's business was for Sangoma to deal with and not for them to intervene.

I learnt from those with unmuted arrows that Kyala was the name of the Sangoma that lived deep within the mountain, although few other details reached me until I came across Cephas.

The teenager advised me I was in dangerous lands, that few strangers come here, and that none usually come seeking Kyala. Cephas says of her - yes this witchdoctor is female, which I was pleased to hear as it fitted in with what I'd already been told of the dark and powerful Thakathi – that she sought out those she wished to use, sometimes through dreams, sometimes through fear and famine and beasts. I take this to mean that she instills obedience by using poisons and riling up wildlife upon the people somehow to convince them that she is powerful. In my mind she is nothing but a trickster, a conjurer using parlor tricks on a primitive people - clearly none of them know of The Magic Circle or have seen David Blane or Dynamo.

I wonder what has happened in this girl's life to lead her to hide herself away bestowing bitter curses upon her own people. Maybe it is the power she thinks she has that has corrupted her.

Cephas agreed to lead me part way. There is a cave, he says, deep and hidden, even he doesn't know where exactly, he just knows the rumours, the stories. The cave is protected by Fumo, but who or what Fumo is I haven't been able to gather. The Inyanga's words were holding up; it gives me hope.

Cephas says I'm not the first mzungu he has met. There have been others over recent months climbing the hills. He seems more open to talking about them as we converse in my pigeon Swahili. I am fluent to a degree, but the language variances are vast as you travel even short distances; you could drive an hour to find that neither English nor Swahili are common tongue but a local dialect completely different altogether. It is no wonder warlords and witches and tribal kings hold such power when communication is limited to the immediate vicinity.

Oil prospectors have been scouting the land, whether they are Rubekki's men or his competition it makes no difference. There is a power play for land and control of the people, and those who have it are trying to keep it and those that don't are trying to obtain it. I've seen it all before. How long will it be before men like me are sent in to clean up the mess, if they're not here already?

I question Cephas about the flower. Dirt and water from the mountain I understand, and instinctively I know this has to be from the cave of Kyala, her sacred abode, but the flower - the mountain forest is teeming with a thousand different species. Life here is abundant. There are more flies and mosquitoes, butterflies and birds, lizards and insects, spiders and snakes, wild boar and baboon, and I dread to think of what else I haven't yet seen. I know there to be elephants at the foot of the mountain and crocodiles and hippopotamus in the rivers. The mountains farther north are famed for their gorillas, but save for the odd grey monkey sitting high up in the trees I had seen nothing as yet that caused my heart to race. But of the flower, Cephas knew nothing. I just had to hope that in the cave it would be obvious.

Cephas says his farewells. He has gone as far as he is prepared to go, whether it's the distance or superstition that has stopped him going any farther I don't know. I thank him and give him a ball of string from my rucksack, knowing it will be valuable for fishing or laying traps. He thanks me with a warning to be careful, "Many do not return," he cautions, but adds that he will watch out for me on the path back down.

With heavy foreboding I press on.

16

My lack of hill walking is showing as I scramble over leaf covered rocks and tread through trickles of water on their way to join the river below that feeds the land running south west. My legs feel like jelly as the incline seem endless and the humidity pushes me back. I want to slice it with my machete, but I know the dense air will only mock me.

I am quite high, nowhere near the top, but deep within the entwined guts as the intestinal tracts of trees wrap a barrier of bark, like a belt hiding a bulging waistband. The light is dimming, too quickly for my liking but there is nothing I can do to prevent the journey of the stars. Up here the birds are silent. Either the air is too thick or something more daunting keeps them away.

I have that certain and intuitive feeling that I am being watched.

I keep walking. I see no one. If there is movement I will see it. I see nothing. If someone is out there I can't hear them either.

The ground begins to level out, shadows deceiving heights of the rocks so that more than once do I stub my boot as I raise my leg. And then I see it.

The wind seems to blow into the crevice sucking me in and then trying to blow me out again as I squeeze through the narrow opening in the rock to reach the wider space beyond that is lit by a single shaft of dwindling light from above. I cling on. If I fall I won't go far, the slope isn't too steep, but the fall would cause a great deal of damage as nothing but sharp rocks hides beneath the boney toes of tree roots that grip to the side of the mountain bowing to the wind.

The wind, that invisible spirit that no man can tame nor direct, breathes in and out deeply so that I can see the leafy trees within fluttering their eyelashes, enticing me in.

That's when I see her. A shimmer of white, a nightdress so familiar, her blonde hair so rich and golden, her pale skin an ivory in such contrast to the family she served with a love so great she was willing to sacrifice all for them. So often I had seen intriguing dark hands running fingers through her golden locks, having never before set their eyes on the likes of fair strands that don't usually dare tread the treacherous path into the jungle.

Enchanted I step forward. With each step I take she steps farther away.

Jenny! I call, uncertain as to whether the words have escaped my mouth or not or whether the echo of sound is only in my head. All else around me blurs. The more I try to focus on her the more my vision seems to fade. *Jenny!* I call again as I breathe in the heavy unnatural mist that fills the cavern that encases the mouth of the cave.

The mist, or is it smoke, I can't tell, it seems to get heavier the farther in I step, seems to suck in towards the cave entrance. It is a narrow opening, or so appears on first glance, until I spot the dark empty socket hiding behind the overhanging branches sneaking a peek at the wider grin of the mouth. I look for teeth but can't see any. Whether my vision is clouded or just my mind I can't be sure, but all sense of danger has vanished.

Jenny skips lightly and unhindered into the looming darkness of the cave, and in my mind I hear her sing my name, beckoning me on to save the children.

The grass leaves shimmer and dance, ghosting around me and spinning me, disorientating me as the garden world before the cave catches in a whirlwind of smoke.

Then I am hit.

I could have sworn one of the trees struck me.

My mind grasps, only briefly, at the idea that the misty smoke, the heavy condensation of humid air that clogs my nose and rests a heavy film on my skin, is nothing less than an hallucinogenic drug designed to deceive anyone brave enough to dare make the climb to knock at the door of the witch, a manipulative ploy to control the foolish visitor. No sooner have I thought this than I am struck again. And again.

Pummelled by the whipping oak branches of living arms that belong to the leaf clad wooden masks of an Entish brood.

Tensing my body instinctively I raise my arms to cover my chest and then duck my chin down and adapt my legs for balance; any pro boxer would have been proud of my defensive stance as I try to tune into who or what is assaulting me.

My back is safely secured, padded by the rucksack that carries my gear. From one clenched fist hangs the machete, loosely pointing to the ground just waiting for instruction.

Slowly the leaves flutter away like birds springing from a cat. They had an advantage at having me blind to their presence, but now I know they are there their courage seems to fail them. Or so I think.

They are men, natives of the mountain and devout followers of the mountain witch. They wear the garb of the forest: the long grass tied on their arms and legs and torso, the painted bark of an ancient tree carved into the face of a demon spirit, branches and horns - some stag, some rhino, bound onto to head pieces that must make maneuvering difficult. Each man, tall and muscular, as though only a prime subject could perform the duty of temple guard, carries a thickened length of twine. At first I think it is bamboo, but as my vision clears I realise it is indeed forest twine bound tightly and treated with sap to bind and toughen its flex. One on its own would be of no consequence, but I counted seven. Now I understood why they had stepped back.

The first whip is flung from a distance I can't reach without a gun, which I don't have drawn. Fortunately, it catches the backpack, but I feel its sharp impact thud and pull away.

A second darts out from the opposite direction. This one catches me on the back of my legs. It doesn't tear the fabric of my combats, but I feel the sting against my calves as I fight to stop my legs from buckling. If they decide to all attack at once I would be done for. I have to close the distance.

Fortunately, they are toying with me, either that or they don't have the nounce to strike me in a united coordinated attack. I reach down with my free hand for the pistol on my gun belt but one of them decides to demonstrate their expertise with their chosen weapon by slapping my hand with pinpoint accuracy. Immediately the back of my hand welts up in a blister as the red line splits the hairs on my skin. I pull it back up to cover my face; a strike there could be permanent, a strike there could cost me an eye.

They are chanting now. It started as a low hum but rises now with their bravado. There are words I don't understand. I can just make out lips moving beneath the masks, and eyes blinking. One eye is normal: brown iris and black pupil. The second eye is blind, an unseeing white moonlit orb. They are creatures of both worlds: half willing participant and devoted follower, and the other half obedient slave. I wonder whether the connection goes both ways, whether if I struck them down she would feel their pain. I hoped so.

The forth strike comes quickly. I don't know whether it was the flicker in the eyes or the draw back of the hand that I glimpsed, but it was enough. I turn slightly to meet it, raising the machete. The rod doesn't break but instead wraps around the blade which I twist in my hand to reel in the fisher on the other end. They had come whale fishing with rods when they should have brought harpoons and I was Moby Dick about to sink Ahab's Pequod.

I pull in the tribesman before he grasps what is happening to him and yank hard on his head in the opposite direction to which his body spun. The crack is audible. I don't let him fall as I hold him up as a shield then try to buy time by flinging the machete at those stood behind me in the mouth of the cave. They duck for cover as I reach to my belt and retrieve the pistol and take aim at any still prepared to cast their rods. One. Two. Three. They drop. I turn for more as the shots ring hollowly about the mountain, echoing back at me, but my targets are fleeing, disappearing back into the woods that hide the cave. A roar bellows deep behind me like nothing I have ever heard before and I realise they weren't running from me. They were running from Fumo.

17

Whether it was the shots that awakened the beast or the fallen protectors that it was bound to I would never know. Fumo, whatever it was, would be bound to her. I wondered whether it had been her checking me out, luring me into the cave, drawing me into her trap using my own image of grief against me. For a moment my heart yearns once more for Jenny, but I have no time to dwell on it, Fumo is coming, I can hear it pounding against the stone and grunting as it pummels the rock. I know what it is only a moment before it leaps out at me from the darkness of the cave.

I see its eyes through the darkness of the cave. White. Pure white. I know it has no mind of its own. It is angry. Ferocious. It is huge!

I've never seen a Silver Back before. Seeing Fumo I can now see how the idea for King Kong had developed, only this was no Kong, more an angry albino version of Mighty Joe Young.

I drop and roll, my backpack catching on a root and pulling me back. That was fortunate. The beast is quick, its reactions sharp. It had anticipated my move and slammed down where I should have rolled to a stand. I jump back, falling on my arse, the rucksack propping me up so that I sit an observer in the circus.

Fumo sniffs the air searching for me. I hold my breath and don't stir a muscle.

I have dropped both the gun and the machete and am weighted to the floor defenceless.

I can see the sharp white teeth, immense in the protruding gaping mouth, part of a thickly covered muscular skull I can't comprehend. Its breath huffs out a heavy mist that stinks foul as though it has been feeding from a sewer. Its fists imprint in the mud as its long pillared arms reach to shoulders the Hulk would be proud of. Its back arches long to a powerful rear that sits on short stumpy legs that could stamp down the wildest of most beasts in the forest. It takes up most of the clearing in front of the cave causing me to wonder just how wide and deep that fissure in the rock runs.

I have nowhere to go, no way of moving, and even if I could it would catch me before I got very far.

It huffs again and then tilts its head towards me and gives a menacing grin. It's funny how even animals can convey mocking emotion. It is toying with me. She is toying with me.

"Jok sent me," I yell, hoping the witch is watching from a distance through the beast's eyes.

Fumo lurches forward suddenly and stops dead in front of me. I flinch but don't jump back - I can't, the backpack has stopped the involuntary movement. Slowly its face edges towards me, bending until its nose is level with mine. I can see the remains of rancid meat hooked between its slightly yellowing teeth, and am close enough to see the reaches of gum decay in patches as it bares its lips back. I hold my breath so as not to breathe in his, all the while taking in, watching and studying the shifting bristles of fur about his head reacting to the leathery twitches of his facial features.

All of a sudden he lurches back and roars. I let out a breath. He thumps his chest hard with clenched fists, exerting his superiority. I unclip the plastic buckles of the backpack and curve my shoulders in under the straps. He pushes off onto his back legs, still bashing his chest. I know what is coming. I roll to one side. He raises his arms in the air and crashes down where I had sat, crushing the rucksack.

I roll two, three times, spinning away as he hits the ground behind me. I grab the gun and roll back towards him sharply. As I had hoped he leaps ahead to where he expects to find me but finds nothing but empty space. I am behind him now. I unload the entire clip into his back.

The great ape falls, reacting to the sharp pain, confused by the needle pricks that have pierced his thick silvery muscles. The bullets aren't enough to kill him, and I doubt they got anywhere close to pushing through to any vital organs.

I find my feet and sprint for the machete. Then dart for the ground closest the cave entrance. He is still pawing with grubby fingers at the tears of blood trickling from his back, craning his neck to try and see what has hit him. I guess he is used to sharp things, twigs, maybe even spears jutting from his flesh, but not bullets; maybe the guerillas had never thought to take it on, maybe they thought best to leave it to her control.

It catches sight of my movement and turns to react as I had hoped. I want the run up.

We run at each other: a locomotive against a scooter. It swings its arms trying to fill the space. I roll to the side, my arms flaying in a purposeful movement, then stand ready to repeat the exchange.

It turns steady, not at first noticing the blood, the tear that carves a smear in its white fur. And then, as though suddenly aware, it flicks its left leg out and watches the blood fly, shaking its head and growling angrily as it breaks into a sprint.

I run wide of the beast as it stumbles forward and falls. I'd nipped its Achilles on the previous run, not enough to cause it major pain but enough to tear on a sudden jolt. I swing the machete low just where I want it, slicing at Fumo's arms as it tries to push itself up. I catch my breath as the great beast tries to stand, then wait till it is almost upright and is turning to face me before I run back and throw myself up in the air with both legs leading, aiming at its chest. I don't have the weight to take it down, I don't need to. Unbalanced on weakened legs it topples backwards, grappling for a handhold as it falls through the gap in the rock where I'd climbed up. I thought it would wedge there allowing me to stab at it, but instead the rock widens under its weight and gives way, its bloody fingers scraping, reaching, grasping for something solid, something firmly fixed to the mountain as it flies back away from it.

I dare to step forward and peer through the gap of broken rock and twisted branches. There is nothing to see. The sound of Fumo bouncing down the rock face rises up to greet me.

<h1 style="text-align:center">18</h1>

I step inside the cave wondering how far I will have to go to find what I need. I am watchful for the rising mist that had confounded me before but here the darkness closes me in. The sun is all but dead to me now and I expect it to be deep into the night by the time I emerge from the cave.

Most of the contents of the backpack are damaged. The jars are broken - I throw them out. The metal water bottle is dented but usable - just. Much had been cushioned by the ropes I'd need to climb down. I find the torch; the lens is cracked but it works. All the glow sticks have been cracked, that is ok, I can still use them to light the way behind me.

I shine light around me. By my feet there are no flowers. I step in further, crouch, dig some clay deposit from the path and scoop it into the bag.

Up ahead I feel the cold breeze of empty space. It is swirling gently, telling me that there is more than one path as the different wind currents collide ahead of me. I will have to choose a path in the dark. How many more there would be I couldn't guess at, but considering the width and depth of the mountain I was now inside I wouldn't be surprised if its tunnels were a labyrinth to rival Moria, though I doubt my host had such a fashion for carving rock as the Dwarves. Whatever caverns opened up ahead of me were likely to be of natural design.

A few steps farther on and I could smell the rot of Fumo's faeces coming from a shadowed space to the left. The path runs up in a gentle gradient. Fumo, I am sure, would have lived alone, but I step cautiously anyway. A thought occurs to me: maybe what makes the cave mud special is the beast that dwells here, maybe the mud sought is his. Holding my breath for as long as I can I shine the torch ahead to the stench. Discarded food scraps are scattered across the cave floor. A dead animal I can't make out is lying torn in pieces, not eaten but dismembered as though it had taken umbrage to its wandering into its lair and had savaged it angrily out of frustration. Likewise, there is a man, dead but not dismembered. He sits there rotting silently as though the great ape had brought him in for comfort and company, a villager that had wandered too close maybe, or who had somehow befriended the beast, or maybe he had been given as a gift to placate the guardian of the holy temple. However he had got there his fate was sealed to rot and be fed upon by the flies and insects that busied themselves in this dead end corner of rock.

I step in as close as I dare and crouch, scoop up some dung and load it in on top of what I have already collected. I don't like the idea of carrying around gorilla crap on my back but in my uncertainty of what is required I am taking no chances.

I backtrack down to the entrance of Fumo's lair and sniff at the second opening. The air is clear, cold and hollow. I can almost taste the empty space on my tongue. I shine the torch in but its beam doesn't penetrate far into the stygian blackness beyond. I draw the beam down knowing there has to be a path. I catch its glimmer thanks to the thin trickle of water that runs down it making its smooth descent perilous. I guess an empty space hangs above and a treacherous fall below. I doubt the path will dry out to allow a firm grip on my boots. This is no tourist trail - no handrails and no warning signs, and absolutely no emergency lighting. I suspect this is a helter-skelter to a watery grave.

I step back away from the entrance to this path and search for another route; there isn't one that I can find. Returning to the slide I beg myself to go slow and easy, fumbling for the cold and moist cave wall, feeling the jagged moss covered rock for balance, hoping it will part for another opening and praying that any troglodytes, either clinging to the walls or scampering on the path, will scatter away from my approach, all the while conscious of the sudden drop on the other side.

The path is steep but not consistent. It rises and falls in jagged breaks as it circles the chimney like a lighthouse stairway. Where the path levels out in places I find myself stood in shallow pools of water which collect from the rock wall and then run off down the other side of the path. I can hear the drip turn to trickle and then to flowing rush the farther down I go, and the farther I go the colder it is getting.

At one of these breaks in the incline I stop to rest to steady myself, taking stock of the situation and the purpose of my trek. Carefully I undo the backpack and retrieve the dented water bottle, fill it from the pool at my feet, and replaced it in the bag. Now I have the mud and the water, but still I see no flower.

I walk on.

19

Leaning against my rock support, sediment settling on my fingers and palm, I can feel the cold air again begin to swirl. Something ahead of my hand scampers away along the wall as my hand brushes it. My hand flinches and shakes away, the involuntary action almost tipping me off balance. A wail of banshees whistles up from the abyss, calling me down. My legs stumble forward as my mind screams to retreat back up to the cave entrance. I put my arm back out to the wall to steady myself once more, the screeching sirens of the wind rising again to blow me back, to slam me against the wall, but the wall is no longer there.

The wailing wind takes me, pushing me farther into the dark cavern that has opened up beside me. I sink into the hole as the path gives way and my senses lose sight of direction as the torch drops from my hand and flickers out.

I haven't fallen far. I'm in but a dip in the path beyond a narrow entrance, the gap in the wall through which I have fallen. My backpack has cushioned my fall and saved my head from crashing against the rock. I roll myself over and fumble about for the torch. More creatures creep and slither away from my fingers. I find the torch, hit the button. Nothing happens. I knock it against the rock. It blinks on. Spindly glutinous legs cower away at speed along with a carpet of fibrous millipede feet marching to the shadows. Pale lidless eyes on anemic furless bodies turn tail and spin up to the path I have involuntary abandoned. I shine the light after them as my mind grasps what has happened. I have found the path I was searching for by accident and am free of the danger of falling to the depths below - I just hope I will be able to see it again in the dark on my way back out.

I can feel the rising wind from the waterfall blasting passed me over my head, telling me a deep straight channel falls back along the untread path behind me. The banshee continues to wail into the distance telling me its depth, but far back my heart sinks as one becomes three high pitched wails as the she-devils splits along different routes.

I pick myself up and begin walking once more, failing to see how any flower can survive in this darkness.

When I reach the crossroads (of sorts) I stand for what feels like an age deliberating as to which way to go. There is a gap in the floor, I assume created by water runoff, which fortunately is too small for me to fall into but big enough to catch my foot in. I am careful to step around it, the thought of breaking my leg down here not appealing. The damp rock, whose sweaty odour rises to fill the void, reflects off my torch beam and bounces light along the narrowing tunnel giving me just enough of a view of the lowering ceiling and stocky walls. Three distinct openings lay before me in a cross burrowed into the rock. All three are foreboding and nefarious. None give even a glimmer of light or a hint of what lays in their guts.

I wonder whether Kyala uses flamed torches or battery powered ones. There is no way she'd be able to navigate this rat run in the dark. I turn my torch to the walls but see no evidence of a wall hanging for a lantern. Then it occurs to me that this is the dummies entrance to her abode. This is the back door. This is the tourist route. She would have an easier way to come and go from her mountain hideout and probably used this just to keep the locals at bay and promulgate her mysticism. She is a tactician, and a devious one at that. I get to thinking how I would go about it as a military exercise, as if I were setting the traps.

How many men would I have lost by now if I'd come with a team? Most I suspect. Too many perils and detours. I have been lucky; it is a word I don't like but in this case it applies. I have been fortunate. I don't believe for a minute that the spiral path leads to a golden coven at the base of its pit. Instinct tells me she wouldn't hide too far down the mountain, where she herself would be entombed and trapped from the world outside.

Luck has led me to this crossway but it's not luck that will get me out. This isn't a hidden underground city filled with orcs or goblins waiting to rise up and pounce from the depths. This is the home of one, a Gollum-esk queen who seeks power over the people and over nature, and for that she needs to be near the surface.

I would have laid detours and distractions to slow my enemy, to lose them and pick them off one by one so that should any get through the odds would be in my favour, on a setting of my design.

I crouch to the tunnel at the head and shine the torch at the ground and then at the roof, the light doesn't go far but it is enough for me to see a slight incline in the gradient of the rock. I step back and check the arms of the other two tunnels - they run flat. I turn and stoop into the head, expecting it to become a crawl space before long.

I undo the pack from my back and carry it loose in one hand, not wanting to be wedged in like a monkey that refuses to let go of the food in the jar. As expected, the path dips and then rises again, worming long to make an undesirable retreat. Soon my space shrinks to a claustrophobic's worst nightmare, but onwards and upwards I crawl, shining my torch ahead to force the skittish creatures to flee from my path. I just hope the batteries don't die on me.

And then the path widens again, and I see a light ahead just as my torch gives up the ghost, dimming momentarily, then flickering manically before blinking out altogether.

My fears had bred in my solitary climb, and more than once I had stopped to control my breathing and racing heart and still my mind from the terrors of imagination and fear of being trapped and gnawed at by unseen hungry insects ready to strip the flesh from my bones. Everything I imagined was multiplied tenfold. So, upon seeing the light I simply clamber out as quickly as possible.

Crawling out, dragging my load behind me with the reckless carelessness of an inexperienced potholer almost falling out from a height having failed to survey what lays ahead, I feel a little foolish.

An experienced caver would have known to look and observe, to judge what was ahead. An experienced caver wouldn't have been panicked by the tight crawl space and lack of light. An experienced caver wouldn't have rushed into an unknown cave filled with trolls and monsters.

I fall about six feet onto a dais covered with fruit and dry flowers cushioning my fall with a dull squishy thud. I am thankful for my soft landing as the backpack falls after me and hits me in the face; if I'd been wearing it it could have acted as a crude mattress to land on, but as it is it hits me hard, the buckle tearing the corner of my brow. I curse my luck for a moment before realising I am relatively ok and that things could have turned out much worse.

I push the pack off and sit up and roll to a seated position and look at my surroundings. I am in Kyala's lair, that much is clear.

I see no sign of the Thakathi but no doubt she is close by, most likely watching me from a distance. She had been linked to Fumo by some strange telepathic connection I couldn't comprehend, the same type of link that binds Benjamin to Daniel Jok, so she will have been alerted to my quest, or at the very least to my trek and trespass upon her domain.

I look at the fruit and flowers stacked up where I sit. They are offerings, most likely left at various points about the mountain for her. This is how she survives: the mountain people provide food to sustain her and provisions to maintain her potions, and in return she offers them healing and protection, throwing in the mix spells of enchantment and vengeance to keep the people bitter and mistrusting of outsiders who could undermine her control over them. It is a simple and primitive ruse, but even I can't deny that some of her power is real, Fumo was evidence of that, and so is Benjamin.

Much of the flowers have survived my fall but I can't distinguish one from another. I am no horticulturalist and know little of flowers and plants. These are of bright colours: reds and yellows, orange and purple, and blues attached to green leafy stems. Quickly I pick one of each and thrust them into the rucksack; they are all flowers of the mountain and if one of them is right then the Inyanga will know.

"Darling are you there?" The voice is hauntingly echoing off the cave walls. It is Jenny, her dulcet tones unmistakable. For a moment I am fooled. It has to be her. There is no way Kyala could know her voice, no way she could mimic it.

"Where are you my darling?" The voice is coming from the source of light, a small opening in the cave wall that I initially took to be daylight, but then reason punches me awake; it is nighttime and dark outside, and Jenny is dead.

I see a flicker of white. A gown? A nightdress? A shawl? It reflects off the lamp hidden far back away from me.

"Come my husband, join me."

I will join her alright, I think as I slide off the dais, but not to fall lovingly into her arms. The primitives of the mountain might be weak minded enough to fall for her charms and manipulation, but I have seen enough of the world to know better.

If the enclosure beyond is her home then I am impressed, not by the comfort (although there is a real lion skin rug and the fur and skins of other animals bedded down about the airy space) but the room smells clean and fresh with sticks burning a sweet aroma that giddies the senses. I try not to breathe in the scents. I admire her cleanliness, wondering how much purification rites play a part in her practice.

Stepping into the light I still see no sign of her. I look to the shadows, the outcrops of rock and boulders, the stubby stalagmites that look like Dorothy's bucket had been thrown, at not one witch but plenty that had marched as a clone army on their foe. I think back to the water in the canister and then dismiss it as nonsense; if only defeating her would be that simple.

Something glints on the floor twenty feet away, drawing my attention. It is a machete. My machete. When had I dropped it? When fighting Fumo? When entering the cave? Had I left it when collecting samples in the ape's lair, or when I fell on the path? I can't remember, and really it is of no circumstance; its presence tells me she has been watching all along. One way or another she has been observing me. Not that I am surprised; if this had been my domain I would have done the same: defended it with controllable access points and observable passageways with hidden pathways only I could access for a speedier route to the stronghold I now stood in. I guessed few made it this far, if any at all. I wonder whether she has contingencies in place should her holy of holies be breached, or is she so confident in her own abilities and power to think she can hold me off on her own? My guess is the later; power mad people have a tendency to leave themselves open, their egos bolstering their confidence beyond their capabilities.

I step forward and bend to feel the fur of the lion, checking it is real. It is. And then I sense rather than see her. She is behind me, having stepped into the doorway along the same path I had just tread. How I hadn't seen or heard her in the other chamber I don't know. Nor do I know how she has crept up so silently, but not so unexpectedly.

I stand, keeping my head low. I don't know how her mind control spell works but I figure minimal eye contact is a safe initial bet to proceed with.

The white gown was hers, the pale skin hers, and I suspect the beauty of her face was too, not that I saw. The pallor of her skin is cadaverous, a pallid shade that almost blends with the loose fabric that drapes her nakedness beneath. The twisted dreadlocks that denote her race echo her heritage but also her power, her eccentricity, and the cause of the obedience of so many. I can see how Fumo had likened itself to her and how she had taken advantage of the beast that shared her intolerance to sunlight and willingness to hide alone in the cave. I have heard of Sangoma's that hunted her kind, albinos, for their skin and blood, believing the properties to be a powerful attribute in their concoction. The blood of an albino is an expensive commodity, and an albino Sangoma a rarity. Now I understand so much of what had turned her bitter and lonesome and why she fought so hard to protect her seclusion, her sanctity.

'Thakathi's mountain, water, earth and her flower,' the old man had said, and now I understand.

Why she steps closer I can't comprehend. Maybe she thinks I am harmless. Maybe she thinks she is impervious, immortal even. Maybe she is curious of my white skin. Maybe she simply wants the company. Who knows? Who cares? I certainly don't as I swing the machete, which I'd picked up when I'd bent down to the rug, and slice at her throat as she draws within distance of my reach. The first strike is a death blow enough to sever her vocal cords and cause her to bleed out in front of me in a gush. The second slash, which comes quickly on the back of the first, takes off her head in a pulsing jet of streaming blood which sprays passed me as she falls to the floor.

Her white gown is sullied, soiled crimson in the dim torch light of the cave, the flames on the wall dancing with a new life as she is struck down.

I reach down and bag the head, feeling like Perseus having slain Medusa.

Now I have my trophy, my cup containing her flower, my flower, all I need to do is get back down the mountain and back to the camp in time to save Benjamin.

<h1 style="text-align:center">20</h1>

It doesn't take me long to find Kyala's secret passageways. They lead a short distance out of the mountain but at a point I don't recognise in the dark of night. Deciding it is too treacherous a trek to risk under the pale moonlight I scurry back into the cave, I'm sure looking like a mouse stepping out to sniff the air before returning to its hidden runs within the walls. Strangely Kyala's cave feels like the safest place rest up.

Making use of her fur coverings I sleep until the cold of dawn awakens me.

The hike down isn't too strenuous. There is a path, a thin line killing growth and flattening the mud telling me of Kyala's regular trails. I follow it down until it meets a stream and then follow the water as it makes its meandering descent to the river below.

Within twenty minutes I have crossed paths with Cephas again. I am pleased to see him. He is surprised to see me. He greets me hesitantly at first, as though I am a ghost; he clearly hadn't expected me to escape the clutches of the gauntlet I faced. Learning that Kyala is dead he is keen to escort me from the mountain. If I were a warrior god strong enough to defeat the witch I was to be feared and revered. Either way, once word gets out there would be outrage amongst her followers and any Mzungu on the mountain would be an obvious target to lash out at.

He leads me down to the river and instructs me to cross. I object. I need my jeep, which I am sure is this side of the river; I remember crossing a small wooden bridge before I abandoned it.

Cephas insists, stating that I have come down at a different place farther round the mountain's wing and that I have to cross here and then follow the river west until it thins out, there I will find the jeep, past the lake and its many tributaries.

"But how do we cross?" I ask, not seeing any obvious signs of a bridge. Even I am not fool enough to wade through waters infested with crocodylus niloticus. I have heard that the giant African reptiles can grow to over six meters and are prevalent in all the waters of the region.

Understanding my body language, if not all my words, he signals to the trees away from the bank where he has a short canoe stowed away from the shore. It is long enough for us both and has one short paddle. Together we drag it toward the water's edge but not into it. Two crocodiles are there waiting for us, their heads just visible under the shallows of the water.

Cephas makes a gesture to indicate that we could carry the boat farther upriver and cross there where it is safer. I concur. We haul the boat back and each take an end just as the trees erupt with life.

A cacophony of chattering panicked calls echoing back and forth tear through the upper branches sending leaves scattering and birds flying. Over excited monkeys swing across toward us, and on the ground bushes part for a score of gorillas knuckle sprinting with lips drawn back and teeth bared.

"Fumo!" Cephas shouts panicked.

"No, Fumo's dead!" I exclaim, suddenly wondering whether Fumo isn't its name but is generic for gorilla. I look back to the clan tearing toward us and then past them. Something big is coming, driving them.

We hesitate no further. There is no other course of action we can take. We lift the canoe to the water, my end going in first. The crocodiles try to snap at the solid butt then curl away in not finding meat to sink their teeth into. I turn back at a loud crunch of bark breaking and am amazed to see the great albino ape burst through the trees.

I jump into the boat, my end sinking heavily in a splash of water until Cephas adds his weight at the other end with a push farther into the river. He is almost in when one of the gorillas closest launches at him and pulls him from the end of the canoe. Both Cephas and the gorilla fall into the water pushing the canoe out of reach of the others on the bank, the crocodiles fill the void between as they rise up on their tails and clamp down on their prey, both human and primate, dragging them down deeper into the water in a bubbling crimson splash.

I back paddle as fast as I can, hoping the crocs don't make a grab for my oar. I can see the gorillas and monkeys stood on the bank staring after me and examining the water they are too afraid to cross. Fumo stands over them, his eyes burning fire, no longer are they the pale servants of the witch, now they are dark, brooding fire and rage, and I am its object of hate.

I cross the river, the whole while Fumo and his servants watching my every move as they attempt to figure out a way across to me. I am safe for the moment. The crocodiles are distracted by the activity splashing on the other side and feasting on yet another innocent bystander to this war I am embroiled in. I exit the boat and run, careful not to let Fumo see my direction; I don't want to risk him shadowing me along the river all the way back to the jeep only for him to catch me there. I needn't have worried. With Kyala lost to him he is as senseless and directionless as the beast he should have been all along.

The river widens to a lake and then narrows again. I find the bridge I had crossed in the jeep, and not long after find the car where I had left it. I keep an eye out for Fumo, but in my heart I know he is still stood staring out over the river trying to find a way to cross over to get to me.

<h1 style="text-align:center">21</h1>

The route back is clear and doesn't take as long as I expected, although speeding away from the mountain I keep looking into my rearview mirror expecting a giant albino silverback racing after me like the T-Rex in Jurassic Park, but Fumo never appears. There is no bursting out from the trees, no gaggle of mad apes screaming from the roadside trying to force me from the road, no angry villagers blockading the dirt track, and no potholes the size of ditches to launch me off course breaking the axle of my only means of transport. The morning is bright, dry, and quiet.

I make good speed, despite giving in to my grumbling stomach. I stop to relieve myself by the side of the road twice to empty the water I had guzzled down when I had got back to the jeep. There had been dried food bars in the rear which I had ignored at first, but having stopped far enough from the mountain I now decide it is safe to rummage in the back for them; I suspect I will need the energy, for there will be little time to hang about once I reach the camp.

It's hard to guess exact distances on country roads with little landmarks, but by my rough estimation I judge myself to be about 10-15 minutes out when I am forced to slam on the brakes of the jeep, letting it settle in the middle of the road idling. I check the surroundings for movement but see none, just the old Inyanga stood stationary in the middle of the road with a blank expression on his face. At first, I think he has slipped into another one of his trances with his eyes rolled back as he leans on his walking stick, but then I realise he is just stood waiting, for me. How he has slipped past my men out of the camp I don't know. How he knew I'd be coming at this point I also don't know. But there is no doubt in my mind that he is there waiting for me, and I know what he wants.

I step out of the jeep, grab what I need and walk the hundred yards or so to where he is stood. He puts out his hand in acceptance of what

I am yet to hand him. I unsaddle the pack from my shoulder and hand it to him without saying a word. He doesn't check it and I don't explain what is in it, I figure he knows as much.

He smiles a leathery grin and begins to mumble a chant as he turns around and walks into the forest and out of sight.

I know in my heart it is the last I will ever see of him and I pray to my own god of war that my faith isn't misplaced. If Mars exists then I hope he's listening, but really I know no god that revels in conflict is a good one.

When I reach the camp I make no mention of seeing the witchdoctor, nor do they make any mention of him being missing. They have other things on their minds, other priorities more pressing.

The boys were still tied up, still blind boys, still viciously growling at anyone and anything that passes by. My heart sinks to see Benjamin in such a state; with the Thakathi dead and her blood, the precious 'flower', handed over to the Inyanga – not so much on a platter but in a bag - I had hoped the curse may have passed by now.

I don't have time to dwell on it. Joshua is out on the front line on the road south of the camp. He has a handful of men with him, but it is never going to be enough. He has engaged with Jok's forward troops, his scouts spying out the enemy territory.

Of course, Jok knew we would have liberated the camp, and he also knew we would be trapped with no way to get the kids out safely. We have two options: stand and fight, or flee through the woods with a bunch of kids programmed and conditioned to turn on us at the first opportunity. It is a cruel game he is playing with us, and I am sure he is revelling in it.

I am not prepared to leave the boys behind, and running with them would be too risky. If Joshua can take down the scouts we could have a chance of blockading the road with their vehicles and slowing the bulk of Jok's forces. I am sure that is Joshua's plan too, especially when word reaches me of the reinforcements being sent.

Captain Akuba is indisposed. No one can reach him. He is on a training exercise somewhere is the presumption being fed back from base. Without him no backup can be authorised. However, hearing our predicament over the radio a unit returning from a border patrol who are twenty miles west of our position have offered assistance. They are thirty minutes out. If we can hold out until they arrive then we might have a fighting chance.

I rally round to Joshua, flanking his opponents, catching them in the crossfire. They fall in the confusion of a single shooter they can't see hiding in the trees, Joshua capitalising on the situation. It is good to see him, and I can tell he is pleased to see me. I just hope he and his men can hold it together long enough to get us through this battle.

The scouts disposed of, we realign the enemy vehicles and strip them of anything useful. The dead men wore army issue bulletproof vests (not that it had saved them from my sniper shots) which makes me wonder what patrols they had come across and robbed. I instruct one of the men to take the vests back to camp and put them on the boys, I don't need to say which ones, they know that Benjamin is to take priority.

I take up position behind the open doors of one of the jeeps as Joshua and the others do the same and there we stand, weapons drawn, waiting for the Mad Dog and his pack of wild animals to come tearing down the road.

22

"Wazimu Mbwa! Wazimu Mbwa!" comes the chant like a train chugging down the track unseen. It is their call of intimidation that starts in a low murmur far away around the bend out of sight of our position. We couldn't make out what they were shouting at first but as they get closer it is unmistakable.

Having been stood in position waiting for some time our nerves are already on edge, even mine. I know we are outnumbered and outgunned.

"Hold," I say gently to encourage the men not to flee. I try saying it calmly and with authority as though I have a plan. I have none. All I can do is hope for the best, failing that, a glorious death.

The chants get louder. Closer.

"Wazimu Mbwa! Wazimu Mbwa!"

"Hold," I say again, glimpsing the sideways glances of my men looking to me uncertainly.

The locomotive pushes on, calling the name of their general to intimidate the enemy they know lays ahead of them. They have no idea of our number, nor even if we are still here guarding the camp, unless that is they can see through the eyes of the blind boys.

Their confidence unnerves me and so does their number. Their march is thundering. The grating of metal clad chain rails rolling, crunching and flattening the dirt road beneath. It sounds like a tank in their convoy.

My mind is bugging - how have they got their hands on a tank?

The first of the troops turns the bend. They are cannon fodder: villagers, adult men with blind eyes loosely cradling AK47's.

More uncertainty.

"Hold!" I confirm a little louder over the din, my voice wavering a touch as my sweaty palms grip at my rifle. I can see regular soldiers mixed in with the villagers, hiding within them and behind them.

"Wait for it. You see the tree on the left with the broken branch halfway, hold fire till they reach it then target Jok's men behind the villagers."

"What if we hit...you know?" asks Abdul.

"Collateral damage," replies Joshua flatly, his tone worryingly disconnected.

They edge forward, a turtle head peering out of the giant shell pulling up behind. It feels like an age before they reach the point I'd indicated but when they do no one opens fire. They are too scared to fire the first shots and I don't blame them, but equally I know if the enemy gets too close ducking behind the jeeps won't save us from the full-on assault.

I take aim and fire.

My first shot misses and clips a villager. He twists back at the impact but keeps on walking without showing any sign of pain at his wound.

I dry my hands on my trousers and take aim again. I can see the enemy begin to raise their weapons. The soldiers break cover to get a clear shot, yelling a command over the shouts of *Wazimu Mbwa!*

My second shot finds its target and my men finally find the incentive they need just as the enemy find theirs.

Bullets rattle off the jeeps as we duck behind them and fire wildly over their shells. The front line of the enemy fall. The next line just walks over them. They will get flattened under the tyres of the oncoming convoy, but I doubt anyone in those vehicles cares too much.

I try to find another soldier to fell, find him and down him. Satisfied I give the signal to retreat, wondering as I do so how far back Daniel Jok is hiding. There is no doubt in my mind that he is in the train, riding a first-class exclusive carriage of his own.

We pull back into the trees, fleeing for the camp and taking fire as we run. We are fortunate not to take losses in that first skirmish as we retreat, using the trees for cover as we duck behind them to fire back at our pursuers.

Only a few chase after us, suspecting maybe that we have booby trapped the trees or have more men in hiding for an ambush. I only wish we had. The bulk of their forces hold back on the road, happy to circle round to the camp the long way.

I know the boys are safe tied to the trees; Jok won't fire at Benjamin if he can help it. I plan to use them as human shields lined up at the trees to the camp entrance, with us behind firing from the huts and towers. It is a gamble, and one I will regret.

There are too many of them. They come through the trees and along the road. We lose our escape route heading north along the road as soon as they turn the corner to block the short driveway through the trees leading to the gates.

"Pick your targets carefully. Don't waste your ammo," is the message I send down the line. We need to prolong the inevitable. I have been in many tight fixes in my illustrious military career, but none as claustrophobic as this. In and out missions, capture or rescue, kill or save, destroy or protect. Those missions weren't personal. They were never my idea. This though is different; a handful of men at my command against an army, human shields, bewitched innocents, and nowhere to run - this scenario is a new one to chalk up in the combat manual. And where the hell did Jok get this army?

It hasn't escaped my attention that these new troops coming at us aren't carrying AK47's. The common villagers, the automatic drones that are walking zombies are carrying the archaic hardware I had expected, but these new recruits, fresh faced and crisp in neatly washed khaki's are carrying M16's, an American assault rifle more equipped for jungle warfare. It is a more expensive weapon and harder to acquire and smuggle in, along with sufficient supplies of ammunition, in bulk. That and the use of tanks makes me wonder what the real bigger picture is here. Who is Jok working for? I know Jok. This isn't his style. He'd become a power hungry, egotistical thug. He had neither the creativity nor the brains to put this outfit together.

The emblems on the armoured jeeps (the ones that had blocked the road must have been pushed aside) echo the shouts of the men that escort them: a crudely drawn dogs head, resembling more a wolf, has been spray painted in black on the bonnet and side of each vehicle, red eyes burning out of the darkness. I can hear the rumble of the tanks, it sounds like more than one, and I have no doubt they are fashioned with the same decor.

Piecing it together I realise Jok has not only lured us here, trapping us, knowing the dilemma we would be faced with in trying to rescue the boys, but he has also left out of necessity. The real purpose of his flight from his main base of operations was to take possession of his new military wing, a privately funded and fully stocked army with which to challenge the national military arm and threaten the government's forces for control. He is seeking a coup.

As the bullets begin to fly my mind slots the pieces together rapidly, knowing I'll have to drop the puzzle to concentrate on saving my own arse. My hope is his troops aren't yet fully combat ready and that he has no immediate strategy in place with which to strike the local forces. For the moment I hope he is driven purely by his hate for me, trying to take advantage of my being in the vicinity with minimal support from the national forces tied up in the capital at the summit.

A bullet whizzes past my head and hits the compound behind me. I duck and snap out of the thoughts sowing a patchwork across my eyes. One of my men takes a slug to the shoulder, not a fatal wound but it sends him back screaming in agony. To my horror the enemy is firing indiscriminately, not caring whether they hit the children. Their lack of discipline is showing through as I am certain this won't have been on Jok's command. He wouldn't willingly risk Benjamin being hit when he knows he can use him as leverage.

I search the trees for my boy, as I feared, he has been hit.

I lurch forward but Joshua catches me and holds me back. He sees what I have missed, what I have failed to recognise. The vest that has been placed on him has taken the impact. His eyes are closed but he is most likely winded and knocked unconscious rather than dead.

My men keep shooting as the villagers are sent forward to untie the children. A foolish move as it creates a separation and an open target to those behind them. I needn't give the order who to shoot at, there is enough fear and hate on our side for each man to judge it for himself.

The first tank wheels into view, its cannon turning, a Dalek screaming *Exterminate* as impatiently it fires. The shell bursts forth in a flame and obliterates the building behind me, sending the few of us sheltering behind the barrels before it flying forward, along with splinters of wood like spears seeking a soft place to land. I can't tell if any of us are seriously injured. My mind is still on Benjamin.

Disoriented I search for him, find him amongst the others by the trees. He is stood, untied, and armed.

And then the tide turns. The eyes of the blind begin to see. The Inyanga, wherever he is, was doing his magic.

Heads shake in confusion, then in uncertainty and disbelievingly, and then angrily. They, both boys and men, recognising their predicament, and ours, turn to fire upon their masters.

The first wave of adversaries fall to the surprise turncoats. There is a moment of stunned stillness, just a beat as bullets continue midflight, the once blind soldiers momentarily self-doubting, their captors-come-sitting ducks confused, and us pleasantly surprised. In that beat a decision is made; those doing the shooting find their confidence to continue their attack; those being fired upon realise they need to take cover; and instinctively I see what will happen next.

"Draw their fire!" I yell, meaning our mutual enemy. It won't take them long to compose themselves and mow down our boys, wiping them off the face of the earth like bird mess from a car windscreen with the use of a water cannon.

"Draw their fire!" I yell again, this time running forward to confront my enemy and protect my war child.

Hesitantly my men follow suit. What I am doing is suicidal and they know it, yet they follow anyway. I'd like to say that we all dodged all the bullets that day, but that doesn't happen in war, only in the movies.

We keep firing as we run, charging our opponents like something out of Zulu in our intent and passion to defend what is ours, but numbering closer to Butch Cassidy and the Sundance Kid in their final frozen frame, certainly acting like them in our last moments of lunacy.

Men in my line drop. So do some of the villagers. To their credit they crowd ahead of the boys to protect them, sacrificing themselves as most fall never to rise up again.

We are lost. Crushed. Defeated. As the slug tears through my cheek, shaving away my jawbone as it slams into my face, I fly back, comforted simply by the thought that we have made a difference in taking some of them out with us.

My rifle spins away as I twist back like a high diver throwing himself off from the ten metre board. My descent is short yet feels slower as the impact of the ground takes an age to hit me. Strangely I feel no pain, just the slop of blood that splashes my now ruined face. Jenny had loved my scars but not how I had got them. She would stroke them, running her finger along the line of the crisscross patch of needlework that adorned my body. She would kiss the sown-up wounds tenderly, sensually, lovingly. In that still small moment as I fall all I can think about is her.

Then I hit the ground with a thump and the clatter of war hits my ears again, and now I think how she would hate my latest disfigurement; so barbaric, so pointless. But it isn't pointless. I'm not fighting for me, nor for money, nor for some higher power, government or otherwise. I am fighting for Benjamin. *Save him!* I hear her say. *Save him!*

I crawl to my fallen firearm and brush off the dirt that has jammed in its nose as it had spearheaded into the ground. A second rifle lays nearby, a loose bloody arm draped over it. I can't see the owner's face, I don't care to know who it is. I push off the arm and grab the rifle, check the magazine; it is half empty. I pull the spare from the belt of the corpse and tuck it into my own, pull myself to my knees and swing around like Rambo firing on all cylinders.

By chance my bullets miss my own men. By chance my bullets miss the boys. By chance my bullets take out a few of the enemy and scatter them briefly to allow the boys enough time to dart for the trees to the left of the camp.

I see Jok then, stood astride a jeep rolling in behind the tank. That is ok, Benjamin is already out of his reach and running through the trees - he is free at last.

I reload the rifles and look for cover. The pain is beginning to ebb into my consciousness. Most of my men are down, including Joshua. I can see him lying in a pool of blood over another man. Both are still. Neither appear to be breathing.

Jok climbs down from the jeep and makes his way into the camp. There is little resistance now, if any. If my men have any sense left they will run with the boys away from the battleground. I don't bother to look if that is the case. This is now between me and him - as it always has been.

Jok is striding forward confidently, ignoring the yells of his men whose cry has changed from one of intimidation and pending victory to one of warning as they come under fire from the west. Better late than never, I think as our promised backup finally arrives. The tank's cannon turns to take aim on a new target too late as it is struck by an anti-tank shell launched from farther along the road. The explosion rocks the troops but not Jok, he strides forward, a steely glaze across his eyes as he ignores all behind him as he fixes his attention on me.

I hear the faint whooping thud of helicopters in the distance beating the air in a rush to get to our position. Someone has finally got hold of Akuba and he has managed to recall our air defences from the capital. Jok's private army is about to die with him.

He holds a machete high, swinging it in a dazzling display, a decadent dance designed to intimidate. I'd seen him do this before. He is predictable. I drop the rifles and pull the dagger from behind my back. It is cliché I know, turn it into a knife fight when I could just shoot him? I could have ended it there, should have done, but a quick death for him was too easy; Jenny deserved better.

His blade swings down from the right as I'd expected. I duck and roll and slice at his hamstring. I miss. With clear vision and intact senses I'd have got my target every time, as I had with Fumo, but my judgement is off, a bullet has chipped away half my face and I haven't accounted for its impact.

Jok swings back down from the left, his blade arcing in a circular motion telling me that its travel will be continuous until it hits something. I have no choice but to roll in the dirt and keep rolling. He steps after me, trying to stab down on my last position, I manage to roll away each time but knowing the open space is littered with obstacles. I hit one, a body, one of the villagers. I can go no farther. I lash out with my knife at his ankles, but he side-steps each obvious thrash of my arm.

The boot of the mad dog falls upon me, pinning my chest to the ground. I look up to see his glaring wild eyes filled with hatred, drool hanging from the mouth of the hound as he bares his teeth and prepares for the death blow to descend as he points the blade toward my trapped ribcage. His arms rise and fall, and I close my eyes for the inevitable end.

I don't hear the running steps, nor the yell I later imagined. All I know is that there is a sudden thump as the air around me changes; air rushing out from the winded Jok; air rushing forward and then away as he is knocked from his feet, the pressure on my chest relieved.

I open my eyes in time to see Benjamin astride Jok having, with the agility of youth, snapped up the fallen machete and is bringing it down on Jok's head. I can see the look of horror on Jok's face, the disbelief. I can see him try to say something, to warn the boy of what he is doing, but it is too late, and he knows it. Instinctively he raises his arms to protect his face. The machete catches his left arm, slices through it and into his shoulder. There it lodges, Benjamin, having exerted all his strength, is not strong enough to pull the blade free. That is ok. It is enough. The wound is deep enough to cause him to bleed out. Let him lie there and die slowly I think to myself as I crawl over and tug at Benjamin to climb off, and then pull him close and then away from the scene. There is still a battle raging and I want to get my boy clear of it.

We run for the trees, hoping, like many of the others who have fled the fight that day, to disappear, to maybe resume a normal life away from the ravages of war.

It is only later as I nurse my wounds, both physical and mental, that I realise that the helicopters I had heard above that final battle were not friends as I had thought, but foe, and that Benjamin and I are part of just a handful of civilian survivors that are still being pursued.

I should have known. I should have seen the signs. I have grown rusty and complacent in my years of peace with Jenny. Seeing the war for what it is has altered the outcome in my mind, but I am too late to go back and change it.

I have many questions. Many doubts. Many regrets. Mostly I wish I'd taken the time to finish the job, to ensure Jok was dead once and for all. If he lives, then he will come after us. I know this as certainly as I know I need air to breathe. I have to take Benjamin and disappear.

THE END
WAR CHILD
Part Two
ATTACK ON THE MOUNTAIN
Coming soon!

If you enjoyed reading this book then please leave a review on my
Amazon page:
amazon.com/author/c.p.clarke
To read FREE short stories by C. P. Clarke go to:
www.cpclarke-author.com[1]

---

1. http://www.cpclarke-author.com

Author's note:

This book is far removed from my previous works. When I started writing it I didn't think it would weave into the wider story of alternate realities that cross over into my other novels, however as I drew toward the end of writing this story there seemed to be a natural way of bringing in an old character and the influence of the mysterious conglomerate controlling the events on the world stage. You'll have to read to the end of part three to see the links in my thinking, but for those who have read my other books, you won't be disappointed.

As for War Child, the concept of this came about as I sat talking to a game designer friend of mine who was looking for an idea for a game based off a novel. As we batted ideas around the table I proposed the idea which led to this book.

Writing the storyline in conjunction with a game designer has been a challenge as the pace of the story has had to keep up with the expectation of playable scenes within a computer game. This has meant that the perspectives of characters has been limited and the action plentiful, all the while trying to maintain a believable storyline.

Fortunately for the storyline, and indeed the original concept, I was able to draw on personal knowledge and experience of the region in which it is set. The whole story is set in Africa, in a non-descript country torn apart by civil war. Into this world of pain is born a boy who must battle his way through the hardships of war and death, the suffering of abduction and the torment of soldiers who wish to use him as a pawn in their own malicious feud.

Very sadly much of what I draw on for this story is all too real in many parts of Africa. Yes, there are elements of the book which are pure fantasy, crossing genres to add elements of battle play for the game with creatures that can't be killed, but on the whole the desperate plight of child soldiers and the brutality they face is very real.

I named this book War Child as it seemed appropriate at the very early stages. It was only once I'd written about a third of the first section that I remembered reading a book of a similar title many years ago before departing for a mission trip to Africa. The book was written by a rapper from Sudan who had found acclaim as an artiste having finally been set free to begin a new life having lived for years as a child soldier. The book is called War Child – A boy soldier's story, by Emmanuel Jal. If you have to decide between reading my book or reading his, then read his! It is an amazing true story that will open up your eyes to the horrors facing some children in Africa today.

I hope you enjoy this story, which for the purposes of the game is set as a trilogy. Hopefully the game itself will follow on day.

C. P. Clarke February 2018

Game storyline based on an original idea by C. P. Clarke and Robert Miller

"Furi'on is the kind of novel that takes you to another place – a place full of suspense and the biggest of twists."
OUT NOW
Visit www.cpclarke-author.com
C. P. CLARKE
FURI'ON
LIFE IN SHADOWS
DAYLIGHT
KILLING
VICKY RIVERS
FURI'ON
POV
POV

Point Of View
C. P. CLARKE
C. P. CLARKE
C. P. CLARKE
POV
POV
POV
A PERSONAL PERSPECTIVE OF THE BIBLE
A PERSONAL PERSPECTIVE OF THE BIBLE
A PERSONAL PERSPECTIVE OF THE BIBLE
now available in digital format or in paperback
visit www.cpclarke-author.com for details

The characters and events portrayed in this book are fictitious. Any similarity to real persons, living or dead is coincidental and not intended by the author.

Text copyright©2017 C.P. Clarke

Game storyline based on an original idea by C. P. Clarke and Robert Miller.

Other titles by the author:
Life In Shadows
Stalking The Daylight
The Killing
Vicky Rivers
Furi'on
Time Locked
Blackout
POV Volumes 1-3
Samuel
A Question of Faith
Stories on a Wall
War Child Trilogy

www.cpclarke-author.com[2]

---

2. http://www.cpclarke-author.com

WAR CHILD 1 ©C.P. Clarke 2017

Don't miss out!

Visit the website below and you can sign up to receive emails whenever C. P. Clarke publishes a new book. There's no charge and no obligation.

https://books2read.com/r/B-A-XCKN-VUIRC

Also by C. P. Clarke

POV
POV
POV 2
POV 3
SAMUEL

Private Peffers
Private Peffers - The Runt
Private Peffers - The Bear Necessities

War Child
War Child - Attack On The Village
War Child - Attack On The Mountain
War Child - Attack On The City

Standalone
Blackout
The Dumping Ground

FURI'ON
Life In Shadows
Stalking The Daylight
THE FALLING
THE KILLING
TIME LOCKED
VICKY RIVERS
DuMAIN